50¢

D0546362

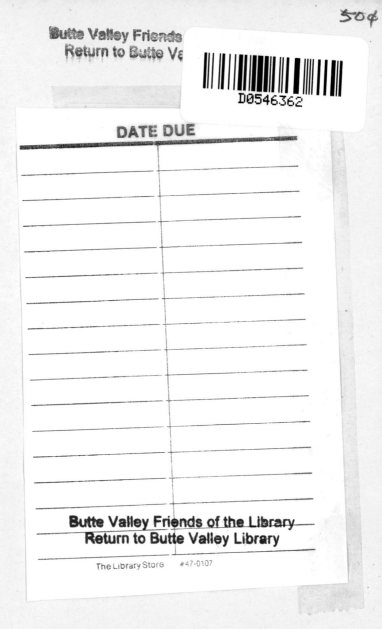

DATE DUE

THE HARDY BOYS ® MYSTERY STORIES

THE SKYFIRE PUZZLE

Franklin W. Dixon

WANDERER BOOKS
Published by Simon & Schuster, Inc. New York

Published by WANDERER BOOKS
A Division of Simon & Schuster, Inc.
Simon & Schuster Building
1230 Avenue of the Americas
New York, New York 10020

Manufactured in the United States of America
10 9 8 7 6 5 4 3 2 1

THE HARDY BOYS, WANDERER and colophon are
registered trademarks of Simon & Schuster, Inc.

Library of Congress Cataloging in Publication Data

Dixon, Franklin W.
  The Skyfire puzzle.

  (The Hardy boys mystery stories)
  Summary: When an important space mission is sabotaged
at Cape Canaveral, the Hardy boys are called in to
investigate.
  [1. John F. Kennedy Space Center—Fiction. 2. Space
flight—Fiction. 3. Mystery and detective stories]
I. Title. II. Series: Dixon, Franklin W. Hardy boys
mystery stories.
PZ7.D644Sj   1985   [Fic]   85-11440
ISBN: 0-671-49732-4
      0-671-49731-6 (pbk)

Contents

1 A Fiery Trap

"Gator Base to Gator One and Gator Two, do you read me?" Frank Hardy asked tensely. "Come in, please!"

But nothing except static crackled from the speaker overhead. The eighteen-year-old ran a hand through his dark hair, flipped a switch to test the power, then waited.

He leaned forward and stared intently at the broad console in front of him. The interior of the van was lost in shadow. Only an eerie, blue-green pulse from the sweeping scopes lit the young detective's lean, athletic frame and the lines of tension in his face.

"Gator One, Gator Two, come *in*, please!" Frank repeated.

Again, only a light whisper of static met his

ears. The digital clock blinked 12:07. A glance at the bright red numbers directly below told him the outside temperature was 97 degrees, the humidity 95. At just past midnight, the Georgia swamp sweltered in summer heat. Inside, the van was a comfortable 77.

"I know you're out there," Frank said impatiently. "Come on, get with it, you guys!" He quickly switched to alternate channel three, then over to nine and back to seven.

"—tor Base, reading you loud and clear now." Chet Morton's voice suddenly boomed over the speaker.

"All right, that's better, Gator Two. Hold 'er on channel seven." Frank let out a grateful sigh. "Gator One, you receiving this okay?"

"Roger, Gator Base," his brother Joe answered at once. "Check me out, will you? I'm making a 'bright eyes' sweep at Sector Two-Niner."

"Got you," said Frank. He made a mental note to inspect his radio equipment thoroughly in the morning. It was probably only atmospheric trouble, but he didn't like electronic problems, especially during an important operation. He concentrated now on the three instruments mounted side by side on the console before him. The radarscope showed a broad eastern sector of the Okefenokee

8

Swamp. The two bright blips were Gator One and Gator Two. Joe Hardy was Gator One. He was three miles away, crouched in a shallow-draft boat with an outboard motor. Joe carried "bright eyes," the code name for their highly sensitive nightscope video camera. Bright eyes captured and intensified light, enabling the viewer to see images otherwise invisible in the dark.

Gator Two was a propeller-driven swamp boat a mile north of Joe's position. Fenton Hardy, the boys' father, drove the swift craft, while Chet Morton operated the "bee-tee," a beeper-tracker device. This advanced electronic instrument recorded heat-radiating targets. If any living creature moved in the swamp, the bee tee would sense it and pin down its location.

"All right, let's move," Frank said quietly. "Make a sweep of Sectors Two and Three."

At once, the radar blips began to drift slowly south. The two boats were running on "whisper power," their engines specially muffled to mask their passage. In the van, the monitor scopes came alive, and Frank picked up the stark red images of the swamp from his brother's bright-eyes camera.

A moment later, Chet's bee-tee relayed a hazy blue glow, like mist. Nothing would appear in it, Frank knew, unless some form of life crossed Chet's field of vision. He leaned back in his contoured chair and waited. Now Gator One and Gator Two were drifting closer together again. Both were nearing a sector of the swamp where murky water passed through narrows shaped like a funnel.

Frank bit his lip. "It's too late!" he muttered under his breath. "We missed him. It should have happened before now!"

He reached up absently and wiped a hand across his brow. In spite of the cool air in the van, beads of perspiration peppered his face.

"Gator Base, I've got a target!" Joe's voice suddenly blurted over the speaker. "It's a boat—small craft, ninety meters south bearing zero-zero-four. He's crossing over, right where we figured."

"I see it," Frank told him, spotting a third blip on his screen. "Gator Two, confirm Gator One if you can. Target is four degrees south-southwest of your position."

"Got it, Gator Base," Chet replied at once. "Confirm single live target. It's man-sized for sure. That's a positive sighting. Repeat—"

"He saw you, Gator One," Frank broke in. "There he goes!"

Suddenly the new blip took off in a burst of speed, leaving the other two far behind.

"Target heading right through the narrows," Frank cried.

"That's where I want him!" Fenton Hardy's voice boomed over the speaker. "Gator One, I have more power than you do. Pull over to starboard, I'm going after him!"

"Roger, Gator Two," Joe snapped. "I'm clear. Come on through."

Frank saw his father's swamp boat streak across the screen. It was powered by an enormous five-foot fan that was enclosed in a wire cage. The boat was designed for high speeds in shallow water; once underway, it could race through an inch or two of water, and even skim over patches of grass and mud.

The craft passed Joe in the dark and darted into the neck of the funnel. The passage was scarcely eight feet wide; Frank had seen it in daylight, and knew the shallow water on either side was thick with swamp grass and the stumps of dead trees. His father, and the fugitive in the boat just ahead, would have to keep to the narrows. If either happened to veer too far to the left or the right, a treacherous snag could rip out the bottom of his boat.

"Gator Two, you're gaining on him," Frank reported, trying to keep his voice steady. "About forty meters and closing fast."

11

"Roger, Gator Base," Chet answered.

"That channel curves left twenty degrees," Frank warned, studying the green scope intently. "You should hit it in about forty-five seconds."

"I've got it on visual," Chet replied. "We're keeping in his wake. He's turning and we're right on his tail!"

"What?" Frank leaned forward and stared at his scope. "He can't be turning yet, there's no channel there!"

"We can see him!" Chet insisted. "He's turning and we're—"

"Chet," Frank blurted, "I'm telling you *there's no passage.* You're too early. He's up to something, fella. I don't know what, but . . . stay on course. Repeat, *stay on course!*"

"If we stay on course we're going to lose him!" Chet blurted.

Mr. Hardy's voice suddenly crackled over the speaker. "This character's found a hole that obviously doesn't show on your scope. But I've got a strong spot on this boat and we can follow him in. He won't get too far."

"I don't like it," Frank answered. "It doesn't feel right. And I've lost him on radar, Dad. That means he's pulled into some pretty thick stuff."

"I'm going after him," Mr. Hardy said

12

flatly. "I *want* that guy, and I didn't come all this way to turn back. Joe, you're the cork in the bottle. If our target happens to slip past us, you'll spot him and head him off. Chet and I can—"

"Dad!" Frank cried out suddenly. "Get out, and get out fast!"

"Huh? What is it, what's wrong?"

Something cold had touched the base of Frank's spine. He came up out of his chair and stared into the scope. "A blip just appeared in the channel about a hundred meters down," he shouted. "It's five times bigger than you are, and it's coming right at you at top speed!"

Joe had heard the transmission and forced himself to stay calm. He laid his nightscope video camera in the bottom of his boat and spoke rapidly into his microphone.

"Frank," he reported, "I can hear the boat now. It sounds like a big cabin cruiser."

"Stay where you are," Frank warned. "Don't try to go in. And Dad, Chet, move out of the way!"

Mr. Hardy had managed to turn his craft around. "It's coming right after us," he said tightly. "We're taking off as fast as we can!"

Suddenly, a blinding white light touched the high swamp grass to Joe's left. The roar of powerful inboard engines shook the night.

13

Quickly the boy started his small outboard motor, twisted the bow sharply and ran the boat into the cover of high grass.

"There's no time to get back to shore," he told himself. "All I can do now is keep out of the way."

Then a new sound ripped the sultry air. Joe froze as the flat, ugly chatter of an automatic weapon tore through the night. They were firing on his father and Chet. *Someone in the big cabin cruiser was trying to kill them!*

"Joe!" Frank's voice grated in his ear. "What's happening, what is it!"

Before Joe could answer, the high, piercing sound of tearing metal shrieked across the swamp. A split second later, a column of searing orange flame licked the sky. Joe felt the rush of heat and smelled the unmistakable odor of gasoline.

Then the cabin cruiser roared out of the channel, its wake nearly swamping Joe's small boat hidden in the nearby grass.

The big cruiser made a tight circle and headed back on its course. Joe could see bits of twisted metal still clinging to the scorched wood of the bow. A man stood stiffly on the forward deck, a coal-black machine gun cradled in his arms.

A terrible, ragged cry of anger escaped Joe's

14

lips, a sound lost in the deep-throated roar of the cruiser's engines. They had deliberately cut the swamp boat in half, hit it so hard the small engine had exploded. Now, they were going back to finish the job—in case his father and Chet were still alive!

2 Deadly Secrets

Joe Hardy didn't hesitate an instant. Jerking the throttle of his outboard motor to full power, he burst through the grass into open water. The cruiser was fifty meters down the channel. Joe could see the bright cone of its spotlight searching the swamp, looking for survivors.

"Joe, Joe! Come in! What happened, what's going on out there?" Frank's voice crackled in his ear.

"Frank, hit the van's siren and don't stop," Joe snapped. "No time to talk. I'm going in!"

Before Frank could answer, Joe tossed his earphones into the bottom of the boat.

Brrrr-a-a-ak! B-r-r-r-raaaaak!

The deadly cough of automatic weapons ripped the air. Joe gritted his teeth and headed straight for the dark bow of the big cruiser. Suddenly, the eerie wail of a siren broke from the north.

"Hey, what's that!" a man called out in alarm. "Cops! Let's get out of here."

"Keep firing," a second voice snarled, "*I'll* tell you when to stop!"

Once more, the automatic weapon churned up the water, cutting the high grass like a deadly scythe.

"Dad, Chet . . . they don't have a chance!" Joe muttered to himself. He was closing in fast on his enemy. Desperately he tore open the satchel at his feet and grasped a black cylinder the size of a tin can. He pulled a string at the base of the can and lobbed it through the air. An instant later, he heard it fall on the deck of the cruiser.

"Wh–what was that?" a voice called out. "Somethin' hit the—"

A moment later, the smoke grenade exploded with a brilliant burst of light. Thick, black clouds enveloped the boat. The men on board shouted in alarm. A burst of fire ripped through the night in Joe's direction. He ducked, then tossed a second grenade and a third. Suddenly, the big engines roared and the cruiser began backing down the channel.

Joe lowered his speed and moved into the

17

thick smoke. "Dad! Chet!" he called out. "Are you all right? Can you hear me? Somebody answer me, please!"

"Over here," Fenton Hardy said quietly. "To your right. We're okay."

Joe breathed an audible sigh of relief. The narrow beam of his flashlight pierced the smoke, picking out two heads poking up through the water.

"Wow, I thought you two were both dead," he said tightly.

"We would be," Mr. Hardy said, "if we hadn't jumped off the airboat before they rammed us. Get us out of here, son, in case those characters decide to try their luck again."

It was close to four in the morning before Frank, Joe, Mr. Hardy, and Chet finished talking to Lieutenant Clark of the Georgia State Police.

"If we'd expected any trouble," Mr. Hardy explained, "I would have called you fellows in. All I knew was that a man who might be involved in a case I'm working on was supposed to be hanging out near this end of the swamp."

Lieutenant Clark nodded. He was aware of Mr. Hardy's reputation. The former crack detective for the New York City Police Department was well known throughout the law enforcement profession.

"I'm afraid we won't find a trace of that cruiser," Clark said wearily. "Or, if we do, the men who tried to run you down won't be anywhere near it. But we'll keep you posted."

"Thanks," Mr. Hardy said.

After saying good-bye, Frank, Joe, Chet, and Fenton Hardy headed north on Highway 84. Frank was driving. "Dad," he said worriedly, "that wasn't just a coincidence, running into those guys."

"No, it wasn't," Mr. Hardy agreed. "It was a setup, had to be. They *knew* we were coming and turned our trap into their own."

Ten minutes later, Frank drove off the highway at the entrance to their motel near Waycross, Georgia. Suddenly, Chet Morton sat up straight and jabbed a finger into the air.

"Frank, douse the lights!" he hissed. "Pull over fast!"

Frank stopped the van and snapped off the lights. "What is it, Chet, what's wrong?"

"Over there," Chet pointed. "There's a car parked in front of our room and two people are sitting inside."

"Chet's right," Mr. Hardy confirmed warily. "It's close to five in the morning, rather late for people to come calling. Let's check it out."

Frank and Joe silently opened the doors of the van and everybody dropped to the ground. Just then a man stepped out of the darkened car and waved at them.

"Hey, Fenton, it's me!" he called out. "Harry Stone."

Mr. Hardy stopped, puzzlement crossing his features. He pulled out the pencil flashlight that he always carried, and shined it at the speaker—a stocky, sandy-haired man in a blue suit.

"It *is* you!" the detective said. He stepped forward and gripped Stone's hand. "Harry, would you mind telling me what you're doing in Waycross, Georgia at five in the morning?"

"Looking for you, as a matter of fact." Harry Stone grinned. "I just—" he paused, catching the tense expression on Mr. Hardy's face. "What's wrong?"

"We've got trouble," the detective said flatly. "Come on, let's go inside. "Uh . . . who's that in your car?"

"My daughter," Stone replied. Then he called, "Okay, Suzanne, come on out."

A slim, attractive young girl with raven-black hair and sparkling blue eyes emerged from the car. She wore blue jeans and a bright red T-shirt. Stone introduced her to the Hardys. Frank and Joe had never met her, but they knew Harry Stone, head of NASA security at the Kennedy Space Center. They had worked with him once before, on the *Sky Sabotage* case.

Mr. Hardy ushered everyone into the motel room, then turned to face Harry Stone.

"How did you know we were here?" he asked.

"I called your wife," Mr. Stone replied. "She gave me the name of this motel. Something's up, isn't it?"

The detective nodded. "We were on a mission in the Okefenokee. It was sabotaged, it's as simple as that. Someone knew we were coming."

Mr. Stone shook his head. "No wonder you were curious about me. Is it okay if I ask what's going on?"

"Sure, just keep it under your hat." Mr. Hardy trusted Harry Stone completely. They had served together with the New York City police before Mr. Hardy retired to become a private investigator. Several years later Mr. Stone had left as well to take the job as security chief at NASA.

"Frankly, I'm not sure where this case is going," Mr. Hardy explained. "First, the president of a major corporation was kidnapped. Then he was released with no ransom demand and no explanation whatever. Later, the offices of a research company were vandalized. But nothing at all was stolen. Two weeks ago, a chemical company in Chicago burned to the ground. There was nothing left of the building."

"Arson?" Mr. Stone asked.

"We're sure of it," Mr. Hardy replied. "But we don't know *why* it was done." He spread his hands. "Frank, Joe, and Chet have been helping me on the case. The incidents are seemingly unrelated, but our computer came up with the names of two or three men who could have been involved in all three events."

"And your clues led you here?" Suzanne inquired.

"Yes. One of the suspects has a sister who owns a fishing camp in the Okefenokee. We found him and were tracking his boat through the swamp, hoping he'd lead us to his accomplices. Then, all of a sudden, we were the ones trapped!"

"And Dad and Chet nearly got killed," Joe added.

Mr. Stone sighed. "You do have problems, that's for sure."

"But how could anyone have known you were here?" Suzanne asked. "We found out from Mrs. Hardy, but we certainly didn't tell anyone else."

"We believe you," Frank assured her. "But there's a leak somewhere. That cabin cruiser and the character with the machine gun didn't just pop up out of thin air."

Harry Stone shifted in his chair. "Fenton, I'm afraid I picked a pretty bad time to ask you for a favor. Looks to me as if you've got your hands full, friend."

"What's up?" Mr. Hardy asked. He shook his head and grinned. "You listened to our problems. We can take time to hear yours."

"We've tried to keep this quiet," Stone said, "but the press knows something is up. The upcoming *Skyfire* shuttle launch at NASA has been plagued with trouble. A rocket booster was damaged, then part of the guidance system failed. A crewman narrowly escaped death when an oxygen test went sour. We can't afford any more incidents. As you probably know, *Skyfire* is scheduled to launch the *Longeye* satellite."

"Hey, I read about that," Joe said. "It's a

big breakthrough in radio telescope technology."

"Right," Stone said. "If *Longeye* does half of what it's supposed to do, it will greatly advance the SETI program—the Search for Extraterrestrial Life." He hesitated, then went on. "It's not generally known, but *Longeye* has some pretty important military implications, too."

Frank exchanged a knowing look with his brother. "Mr. Stone, if these problems are just . . . *accidents*, why are you involved? Where does NASA security come into the picture?"

Stone gave Frank a sober look. "You hit the nail right on the head, son. That's just it. I don't think they're accidents at all. I'm certain someone's deliberately trying to stop the *Skyfire* launch."

"What?" Frank stared. "If that's true, then—"

Frank's words were cut off abruptly as a high-pitched buzzing sound came from Harry Stone's jacket. "Someone's trying to reach me," their visitor said, punching the beeping device to silence.

Suzanne stood up. "I'll check in on the phone in the car." She moved quickly to the

24

door and disappeared. Moments later, she rushed back into the room. Her face was pale, her blue eyes wide as saucers.

"They want you back at NASA at once," she gasped. "There's been an explosion at the space center!"

3 Space Bound

Frank, Joe, Chet, and Suzanne raced steadily along Florida's eastern coast in the Hardy's black van. Mr. Stone had left Waycross shortly after sunup in a special helicopter NASA had sent to pick him up. Mr. Hardy had chartered a flight to Miami in an effort to tie up some loose ends in his own baffling case, and had promised to meet the young detectives at the space center later.

"Hey, the water looks great," Chet Morton exclaimed. "I hope we'll have time to get in some swimming."

"That's Mosquito Lagoon to your left," Suzanne pointed out. "And the strip of land past it is the Canaveral National Seashore. Beyond it is the Atlantic—" She stopped, threw back her head, and laughed. "Why am I giving you guys the tour? You've been all over space country before."

"It's great to be back," Joe declared. "The Cape's an exciting place to be."

"A little too exciting right now," Suzanne said somberly. "My dad's really worried." Her blue eyes clouded and she swept dark hair out of her face. "Whoever's behind this business is striking directly at the *Longeye* project. If anything should happen to that radio telescope—" Her words trailed off and she stared straight ahead into the sun.

Frank, who was behind the wheel again, glanced over and smiled at Suzanne, who, at seventeen, was a year younger than he. The dark-haired detective had taken an immediate liking to the attractive girl, and it disturbed him to see her so troubled.

"Look," he said, "we have some experience with sabotaged satellites. That's why your father suggested we come to the space center and work on this case. We'll do everything we can to help."

"We have a whole van full of guaranteed 'crook catching' devices," Joe added with a grin. "Of course, we didn't do so great last night."

"From what I understand, there wasn't much you could do," Suzanne pointed out.

"Frank gave me a guided tour of the van before we left this morning. I'm really impressed. Where did you get it, anyway? I never saw so much high-tech equipment outside of the NASA control center."

"Well, of course we're not that good," Frank said wryly. "But we do have some pretty advanced hardware."

"To answer your question," Joe said, "the van was a gift from the Bayport Police Department. We recently solved a case in Africa and received award money. We donated the prize to one of the police charities, and the department gave us the van as thanks."

"It was surplus equipment," Frank explained. "It came with a complete computer setup, a radio communications center and a lot of protective devices. We've done some customizing ourselves, and added a few surprises."

"Oh?" Suzanne raised a curious brow. "What kind of surprises?"

"You'll see sooner or later," Frank grinned. "If we told you *everything* now, it wouldn't be a surprise, would it?"

Early in the afternoon, the van crossed the NASA Causeway and headed for the John F. Kennedy Space Center. Suzanne's father met them at the security gate in an open electric car. With him was his top aide, Lew Gorman, a slim young man with dark, brooding eyes and a shock of unruly black hair. Frank guessed him to be in his late twenties.

"It looks as if things are going from bad to worse," Mr. Stone reported glumly. "My boss, Maxwell Grant, is hopping mad about this latest episode."

"I think we've met him before," Joe said. "He's deputy director of operations, right?"

"Right," Stone said. "Max is a great guy, and I don't blame him for his concern. We're all concerned!"

"It's not Grant who's stirring up trouble for us, Harry, and you know it," Lew Gorman said tightly.

"Oh? Who is, then?" Joe inquired.

"Nat Cramer and Pete McConnel," Mr. Stone replied. "They're both at the explosion site now, and you'll meet them as soon as we get there. Cramer's the project specialist for the Starglass Corporation, the company that developed *Longeye*. Cramer's all right, I guess, but McConnel's a big pain in the neck. He's Cramer's security man, a big bully. He and I don't get along at all."

"Pete McConnel doesn't get along with his own dog," Gorman said dryly.

The electric car came to a halt outside a

three-story research building and they were met at the door by Maxwell Grant, who greeted them warmly. He was a stout, affable man in his early fifties. White hair fringed his balding head, matching a full mustache under his hawklike nose.

"I guess Harry's filled you in," he said, ushering them quickly down a long, brightly lit hall. "We're up to our necks in trouble. The *Skyfire* launch has been jinxed from the start."

"Sir, just when is the launch supposed to take place?" Chet asked.

"We're scheduled to lift off on the twenty-first," Grant told him. "That's less than a week away. If things don't get straightened out fast around here, we may *never* get that bird off the ground."

He slid back a heavy steel door and led the way into a high-ceilinged, cavernous room. Two men standing nearby turned to face them. From Stone's description, it was easy to tell Cramer from McConnel. Cramer was a tall, unusually gaunt man in his thirties. Thick-lensed glasses made his eyes look owlish. Pete McConnel was built like a lineman. His hair was cropped nearly to his skull, and he had the nose of a prizefighter. When he spotted Harry Stone, his lips tightened into a sneer.

"Well, well," he grinned, "if it isn't NASA's ace security man, come to pay us a visit."

Harry Stone tightened his fists but held his temper. Maxwell Grant stepped forward and introduced Frank, Joe, Chet, and Suzanne. McConnel nodded a curt greeting, and looked the Hardys over from head to toe.

"I've heard about you guys," he said coolly. "Bringing in outside help to solve your problems, are you, Stone?" He threw back his head and laughed. "That's great. Harry Stone's baffled, so he's called in a couple of kids!"

"If you've heard of the Hardys before," Grant said evenly, "you know they're seasoned investigators, Mr. McConnel. They've proven themselves a dozen times over—and here at NASA, too, by the way."

"Hey, I'm not complaining," McConnel grinned. "Whatever ol' Harry needs." He turned and walked across the big room toward the hall.

"You'll have to excuse Pete," Nat Cramer said quietly. "He means well, but he gets a little carried away. Uh . . . if you're interested, I'd be glad to show you fellows where the explosion occurred. It's right over there."

"We'd like that very much," Frank told him.

The Hardys, Chet, and Suzanne followed Cramer, who led them around a high canvas screen that had been rigged around the site. Mr. Stone and Lew Gorman stayed back to talk to Grant.

One look at the area told the young detectives what had happened. Intense heat had turned the concrete floor stark white. Within the blast area, the remains of metal equipment were welded together and partially melted in puddles on the floor.

A few yards away, two identical devices stood side by side behind a low concrete wall. They were cylindrical in shape, nearly four feet high, and covered by a sheathing of gleaming chrome and stainless steel.

"We were lucky," Cramer said. "Pete believes whoever was responsible for this used a shaped incendiary charge, but apparently wasn't familiar with that type of explosive. The concentrated force of the blast missed it's target—the *Longeye* research area."

"Mr. Cramer," Frank asked, "why are there *two* satellite packages here? Is one a backup system?"

"Oh, no," Cramer said hastily. "One of the *Longeye* devices you see here is a working mock-up. It contains the same microcomponents as the actual device, but it's not, ah . . . *space reliable*, as we say. The mock-up lets us try out design modifications without going to the time and expense of working on the real thing."

"And which is the real telescope?" Chet asked.

Cramer showed him a broad grin. "Why, the one that weighs 278 pounds less than the other one."

"Oh. Well, that explains it," Chet said dryly.

"I've got to run now," Cramer said. "I'm sure I'll bump into you all later." He turned and stalked quickly across the concrete floor.

"Scientists," Chet said gruffly. "They sure don't like to give away any of their big secrets!"

"Lift 'em both," Joe advised. "He told you how to get the answer."

"Swell idea," Chet said. "I'll go out and get a crane."

Maxwell Grant was waiting for them behind the canvas wall. Harry Stone and Lew Gorman had already left.

"Let's walk back outside," Grant suggested. He grinned broadly at the four. "I've got a piece of news I think you'll find to your liking."

"Great, we could use some good news," Joe said. "What's up?"

Grant didn't answer. When they were out of the building in the bright Florida sun, he turned and faced them again. "Maybe you're familiar with NASA's new policy," he said. "Civilian personnel such as teachers and students are now being included on some shuttle trips. I received word this morning that our passengers scheduled for *Skyfire* canceled out. If you four would like to be considered as replacements, I'd be glad to recommend you."

"Hey, would we!" Joe shouted, "that's fantastic!"

"A trip on *Skyfire?*" Suzanne added. "Un-*real!*"

"There are a few preliminary tests involved," Grant went on, "but nothing that'll give you any trouble. I'll get in touch with you first thing in the—" He stopped as a raucous shout went up behind him. "Uh-oh," he said, "here comes trouble again."

They all turned as Pete McConnel jogged around the side of the research building. His broad face was flushed, and his jaw was set like a bulldog ready to bite.

"Okay, Grant, take a look at this!" he snapped. He stopped directly in the deputy

34

director's path and shoved a wad of gray material under his nose. "Your so-called *security* experts spent all morning going over the explosion site," he said sharply. "Only they didn't find this!"

"And just what is it you're talking about?" Grant asked coolly.

"It's a piece of plastic explosive," McConnel crowed. "I know explosives from my days in army intelligence. Unless I miss my guess, this particular sample was manufactured in one of the eastern bloc nations. You've got a Communist spy here at NASA right under your nose, Grant, and Harry Stone's too dumb to do anything about it!"

4 Dark Intruders

"It's working fine," Joe Hardy called out to his brother, who was sitting in the open van near the beach. "I have the hang of it now." He kept his eyes on a small craft circling the beach, while his fingers played deftly over the miniature controls. Turning a switch slightly to the left, he banked the plane toward the ocean, dipped its wings low over the waves and sent it whining into the air. The radio-controlled biplane, *Blackhawk*, had a wing-spread of only twenty-eight inches. Still, etched against the darkening sky, it was easy to mistake it for a full-sized craft.

"You getting anything," Joe asked, "any kind of a reading?"

"I'm tracking you," Frank answered, "but

that's all. We'll have to try the bright eyes gear after dark." He looked intently at his console of scopes and dials. Chet Morton leaned over his shoulder, checking off readings on his clipboard. The van was parked on a sandy road between the beach and the small house the Hardys had rented south of Cape Canaveral. The sun was beginning to set behind them and left a warmish glow over the Atlantic.

"I'm bringing her back," Joe said. "Fuel's running low, and these offshore breezes are a little tricky."

Banking the *Blackhawk* into a wide arc, he lowered the throttle control slightly and turned the craft into the wind. A curious seagull followed the plane, squawked an angry challenge at the unfamiliar bird in its neighborhood, and flapped off over the water. Joe brought the plane in gently, let it hover above the smooth stretch of sand for a few seconds, then eased it to the ground.

"Hey, great landing, ace!" Chet Morton applauded from the door of the van. "You're getting pretty good."

"Yeah, I imagine Major Halman will want me to help him fly the shuttle," Joe said dryly.

Chet laughed as he and Frank stepped out

of the van and watched Joe retrieve the plane. The younger Hardy checked the *Blackhawk* carefully, then set it on the floor of the vehicle.

"I think it'll work fine," Frank said. "We'll test the bright eyes after dark. Does the extra weight of the mini-video camera give you any trouble?"

Joe shrugged. "It was a little nose-heavy at first, but I know how to work around that."

"Great. If we can really get night vision from above, it'll add a whole new dimension to our search-and-detect setup." Frank glanced curiously at Chet. "You're our engine man. Think you could do anything about working up a whisper mode for the *Blackhawk*? It sure makes a lot of noise."

"I can give it a try," Chet said thoughtfully. "Silent running's going to cost you more weight, though. Even if we're talking about ounces, that might affect the plane's flight."

"I know," Frank agreed. "Well, give it some thought." He turned as a car pulled up at the beach house. "Hey, we've got company. Looks like Mr. Stone."

"And Suzanne," Joe grinned. "You forgot to mention her."

"I didn't forget at all," Frank said solemnly.

"I, uh, just didn't notice whether she came or not."

"Oh, sure you didn't," Joe said, teasing his older brother.

"Why don't you make sure *Blackhawk* doesn't bounce around back there?" Frank suggested. "This road's a little rough."

"Aye, aye, cap'n," Joe said, enjoying his brother's discomfort. He stepped into the rear of the van and lifted the plane into its snug compartment. There was a storage unit for special equipment, rigged just above the three black dirt bikes fastened securely to the right-hand wall of the van.

"Ready to go," he called out to Frank as he slid the side door shut.

Frank started the engine and jerked the van quickly into gear. Chet was sitting beside him.

"Hey, take it easy!" Joe said from the back. "Suzanne'll still be there, buddy!"

Frank muttered under his breath, but did not answer. Instead, he drove off to meet the Stones.

Minutes later, the young people and the security chief were gathered in the cabin's living room.

"Maxwell Grant understands the problems

of security at a setup as big as NASA," Mr. Stone said, "but this thing has put him under a great deal of pressure."

"I suppose a lot of that pressure's coming from Pete McConnel," Frank spoke up.

"Right. McConnel isn't helping any, I can tell you. The Starglass Corporation carries a lot of weight at NASA. Darn it all, anyway." Stone's face clouded and he slammed his fist angrily into his palm. "My security team went over the explosion site with a fine-toothed comb. McConnel coming up with that piece of plastic explosive really made me look stupid. We should have found it, there's no question about that!"

"Do you agree with him?" Joe asked. "Is the sample from one of the eastern bloc countries?"

"The lab's got it now, and we should know for sure in the morning. But I don't doubt that McConnel's right. I don't like him, but the man knows his business."

"Then a spy may have penetrated NASA," Frank said soberly.

"People who work at the space center are checked and double-checked, back to the day they were born," Stone said wearily. "But yes, it's possible. Anything's possible in this business."

"Dad, it's going to work out," Suzanne said softly. "I know it is."

"Thanks, honey." Stone reached over and squeezed his daughter's hand. "I wish I were as confident as you are."

The Stones stayed for dinner and Mr. Hardy arrived just in time to enjoy the delicious pot roast Chet had prepared. Afterward, everyone went outside to the patio behind the cabin to take advantage of the pleasant offshore breeze. A string of white lights outlined a cruise ship far out on the Atlantic. Mr. Hardy stared at it glumly.

"Fenton, you're awfully quiet," Harry Stone said. "I take it your day wasn't a whole lot better than mine."

"Miami was a dead end," Mr. Hardy replied, "a waste of time. The police told me that the man I wanted to find had skipped town. He has contacts in St. Petersburg—a guy he'd served time with in Atlanta. I'll have to try to find him in St. Pete." The detective raised a brow at Frank and Joe. "I can't prove it, of course, but I'd bet my last dollar I know why he wasn't in Miami."

"Because he was one of those characters who tried to gun you down in Georgia last night, right?" Joe said.

"Exactly." Mr. Hardy shrugged. "There are

two, maybe three, men that could have been involved in the chemical company fire. And one of them served time for kidnapping before."

"Which means he's a likely candidate for the abduction of that corporation president," Frank finished.

Fenton Hardy sighed and looked sourly at the dark horizon. "It doesn't do a whole lot of good to tie them all together. I still don't even have a motive for the crimes!"

"I have an idea," Mr. Stone said and stood up. He grinned at Mr. Hardy. "You and I can trade cases."

The detective laughed. "Neither one of us would be any better off than we are now," he said.

The Hardys and Chet escorted the Stones to their car.

"I'd like to stay longer," Suzanne whispered to Frank. "But Dad's had about all he can handle for one day. It's been rough."

Frank put an arm around her shoulder. "It'll work out," he assured her. "He'll get a break real soon."

After the Stones had left, Mr. Hardy decided to take a walk along the beach. "Are you guys going to get some sleep?" he asked. "You need to be alert for the shuttle flight training tomorrow morning."

"I don't think any of us can sleep," Joe told him. "Besides, we want to test the *Blackhawk* in the dark. We may discover something around here that'll give us a clue to the mystery."

Mr. Hardy grinned. "Okay. See you later, then." With that, he disappeared behind the house and went toward the beach.

Frank, Joe, and Chet drove the van a hundred yards down the road, looking for a spot to try out the *Blackhawk*'s night vision capabilities. Joe took care of refueling, while Chet ran a circuit check with Frank, making sure the tiny video camera in the belly of the plane was sending a steady signal to the scope in the van. When they were ready, Joe climbed atop the van for a better view, carrying his compact radio controls. He wore a headset and mike to keep him in touch with Frank inside.

"Ready when you are," Joe said.

"Take off," Frank told him. "We're all set."

Joe's fingers worked the controls, and the *Blackhawk* whined swiftly into the air. Keeping the plane steady and under control at night was tricky business, a lot like instrument flying in a full-sized craft. As long as Joe could see the amber-colored light atop the tail he was all right. If he lost sight of the light, he was in danger of losing the plane itself.

"Bright-eyes is coming in fine," Frank reported from the van. "I can see the dunes and the edge of the beach . . . the waves coming in show up as lighter shades of red."

"Great," Joe said, "I'm circling back now, otherwise I may lose it. If we want more range on this baby, we'll need a brighter light. Maybe a mini-strobe would do it."

"Hey," Frank exclaimed, "bank to port a little. We've got Dad down there on the beach. There, that's it. Can you come in lower? Yeah, now he's spotted the plane. I've got a nightscope image of him waving!"

"I'll try to make another pass," Joe said. "Give me a corrected heading when I come back around." He guided the *Blackhawk* down the beach, banked tightly and circled for a second run. The amber light streaked through the night and dipped low over the dunes.

"Steady," Frank's voice crackled in his ears. "You're too close to the water. Come left three degrees. Okay, keep her right there . . . you ought to be ab—Joe!" he suddenly shouted. "Come around quick, cover that stretch again!"

44

"Huh? What's up?"

"Just do it," Frank snapped. "Hurry!"

Joe shrugged and squinted into the dark, then circled the *Blackhawk* back along the course he'd covered before.

"There, straight ahead," Frank prompted, "it ought to be right over—Joe, I was right—" His voice dropped. "There are three men down there, running behind the dunes—*and they're headed straight for Dad!*"

5 G-Force!

Joe's stomach tightened into a knot. He swept the *Blackhawk* in a circle, bringing it whining back toward the van. A harsh, strident sound cut through the night as Frank gave three quick blasts on the van's powerful air horn, a danger signal their father would know at once. At the same time, he blinked his headlights, then hit the horn again.

"Chet," Joe shouted into his mike, "get on the spotlight, see if you can find 'em!"

"Right," Chet answered.

A bright cone of light stabbed through the darkness. From the passenger's side of the van, Chet moved the spot on its swivel mount, turning the grassy dunes stark white.

"Left," Joe prompted, "higher, Chet, closer to the beach—"

Suddenly, the beam caught a dark figure running. The man stopped, frozen in the circle of light. One hand came up before his eyes, the other pointed a stubby black weapon at the spot. Smoke hid his face as a thunderous explosion shook the night. Lead whined dangerously close to Joe's head.

"He's firing at us," Frank yelled.

"Don't tell *me*," Joe said tightly, "I nearly caught that shot between my teeth!"

The gunman fired once more. The muzzle blast was a deep, throaty roar, the unmistakable sound of a heavy-caliber pistol. Chet's spot didn't waver. The man paused another instant, then turned and disappeared over a grass-covered dune.

"Keep on him," Joe urged, "keep on him . . . there! Ten yards right. Hey, the other two are with him!"

He could see them plainly now, three black-clad men in skintight clothing, black ski masks covering all but their eyes. They ran low, darting through the dunes a few feet apart in a classic combat attack. Joe's skin crawled. *"Where's Dad, where is he? What's he doing?"*

Suddenly, Joe saw him sprinting away from the open beach toward the cover of the dunes farther north. His assailants spotted him, too. One shouted and pointed in Mr. Hardy's direction. The others raced north while the first went to his knees, gripped his pistol before him in both hands and squeezed off three quick shots. Joe held his breath as Mr. Hardy dove for cover, rolled and came up running.

He'll never make it, Joe thought desperately, *they're too close, they'll cut him off—*

Twisting the controls between his fingers, he banked the *Blackhawk* in a tight, tortuous curve, then let the plane streak low across the beach.

"Don't lose 'em, Chet," he called out, "keep them in that spot!"

Chet shouted an answer, but Joe didn't hear. He brought the plane in on full power, less than three feet above the sand. The small engine snarled through the night. Just then, the armed men closed in on Mr. Hardy. As one raised his weapon to fire, his companion shouted a warning. The gunman jerked around and stared, then cried out in alarm and leaped for cover as the *Blackhawk* came at him like a missile.

Joe shot the plane straight up, praying the wings wouldn't snap. The tiny engine sputtered, then held. Joe followed the streaking amber light, banked the plane sharply and sent it screaming down again.

Chet pinned the black-clad assailants in his beam. Joe's plane whined like a hornet, buzzing dangerously close to their heads. The gunmen paused, glanced up the beach and then scattered. Joe heard the wail of a siren, saw the flashing red and blue lights of a police car and knew Frank had called for help. The car left the road and bounced precariously over a dune, heading for the open stretch of beach.

Frank and Chet were out of the van, racing toward the water. Joe brought the *Blackhawk* winging back, and set it down on the road in a hasty landing. Turning, he heard the protesting howl of tires and saw the squad car had foundered in heavy sand.

"We lost 'em again," Joe muttered angrily under his breath. "Those guys are experts at squirming out of trouble!"

Early the next morning, Frank and Suzanne were returning from the NASA space medicine center where they had just completed exhaustive pre-flight physicals. Joe and Chet had finished first, and promised to meet them at the centrifuge lab for the next round of tests.

"Dad's really fuming," Frank said. "He was up all night, and when we left he was still on the phone, calling his contacts all over the country. He says at least last night's attack proves he's on the right track."

"I guess he's right," Suzanne sighed. "If he wasn't turning over the right rocks, they wouldn't be trying so hard to get him out of the way." She looked at the big building ahead and made a face. "I'm not at *all* sure I'm ready for this. Spinning around fast isn't my idea of a good time."

"Hey, come on," Frank told her. "They say the centrifuge test isn't any worse than a really fast ride at the fair."

"I know," Suzanne groaned. "You know what *I* do at the fair, Frank Hardy? I eat hot dogs and cotton candy and watch *other* people scream on those rides."

Frank laughed. "I guess we're all going to get to watch *you* scream, now."

"Oh, that's funny," Suzanne said flatly, "really funny."

Chet and Joe were waiting inside the NASA centrifuge lab, along with a man in a white jacket who introduced himself as Dr. Hal Carter. Dr. Carter issued skintight flight suits to the young people and showed them where to change. A few moments later, he led them through a door to the centrifuge itself.

Suzanne gave the device a cautious inspection. It was a circular room with an enormous axle mounted in its center. A long metal arm led from the axle to the small, bullet-shaped centrifuge cabin at its end.

"Oh boy," Suzanne said dryly, "I can hardly wait."

"It's not all that bad," Dr. Carter told her. "Really." He turned to face the group. "I assume you know a little about gravity, but you get to hear my standard lecture anyway." He grinned and went on. "A simple definition of gravity is the force exerted by a body such as the Earth. We feel that force as a weight, a pressure. Everyone, no matter what he weighs on the scales, feels one gravity, or one G of that pressure. Two Gs is twice your weight, and so on.

"You've all felt the pressure of slightly increased Gs taking off in a plane, or going up fast in an elevator. This machine," Carter explained, nodding toward the centrifuge, "enables us to simulate the effect of the acceleration and deceleration experienced during the launching and re-entry phases of space flight."

"Uh, just how many Gs will we feel in that thing?" Chet asked.

"You'll only experience two, or possibly three, Gs on the shuttle launch during liftoff, and that won't last more than a couple of minutes. We'll take you higher than that on the centrifuge, but only for very brief periods."

Chet did some quick arithmetic in his head. "Those Gs better come off fast when I get out of that thing," he said darkly. "I'm trying to *lose* weight. I don't need four or five times what I've got."

Dr. Carter laughed. "We've never had anyone hang on to their Gs yet. Come on, let's get started. One at a time."

Moments later, Joe Hardy was strapped into the centrifuge capsule, protective straps laced snuggly about his body. He was attached to sensors which would monitor his blood pressure, respiration, and heartbeat during the test. While Joe was being prepared, Chet Morton snapped pictures of the proceedings with his mini-camera.

"We'll watch you from the observation window," Dr. Carter told Joe. "And those two men behind that other window," he pointed, "will control the centrifuge."

"Will I be able to tell how many Gs I'm experiencing?" Joe asked.

"The digital display in front of you will register your Gs. By the way, that lens at eye level is a TV camera. We'll be able to observe you during the test, and of course the technicians will be watching you at all times, too."

"That's good to know." Joe forced a grin. "I guess I'm ready if you are, doctor."

Carter made a final check of the capsule, locked the hatch, and led Frank, Chet, and Suzanne back to the observation room. The small chamber next to the control room was equipped with theater-type seats, a TV monitor, and intercom equipment.

"All right," Dr. Carter spoke into his mike, "let's go, Tom."

"Test commencing, doctor."

With a deep hum of power, the centrifuge began to rotate slowly about its axis, gradually picking up speed. In moments, the capsule was whipping rapidly past the observation window.

"Two Gs," a voice droned through the speaker. "Two point three . . . two point seven . . . three Gs—"

Suzanne Stone leaned forward intently, unconsciously gripping Frank's arm. "He seems okay," she said nervously. "Is he feeling anything yet, Dr. Carter?"

"Oh, yes. You feel the extra pressure at once. He'll begin to get a little uncomfortable any moment now. There, look!" He pointed to the monitor. Joe's head was pressed firmly against the padded back of the seat. The flesh on his face went taut; his lips drew back, baring his teeth.

"Is he all right?" Suzanne asked.

"Perfectly all right," Dr. Carter assured her.

"Four point seven," the technician called out. "Five Gs . . . five point three—"

"He can feel pressure against his eyeballs now," Dr. Carter said, "and a tightening in his chest. Pressure pushes blood away from the heart. Joe weighs 155 under one G. That means he is now experiencing 821.5 pounds."

"Wow," Chet sighed, "and I thought I had a problem!"

"They'll take him up to seven, seven point five. That's all that's necessary for shuttle testing," Dr. Carter said.

"What's the danger point?" Frank asked. "How many Gs can a person take before—"

"Before body damage is sustained?" Dr. Carter finished. "That depends on the individual, of course, and on the duration of a particular amount of Gs. The Mercury astronauts sustained seven Gs upon re-entry in 1962. Ham, the chimp, took sixteen Gs atop a Redstone rocket in 1961. He apparently experienced no ill effects, but I wouldn't care to—" Dr. Carter stopped, frowned at the digital readout and spoke quickly into his mike. "Tom, you're edging up to seven point eight," he said irritably. "Are you guys asleep in there?"

No one answered. The speaker overhead remained silent.

"Tom," Dr. Carter snapped, "are you reading me? What's going on in there!" He glanced at the readout above Joe's TV monitor. The red numbers blinked 8, then rapidly increased to 8.7.

"Dr. Carter, what is it?" Frank asked.

"I don't know but I don't like it." Carter jumped out of his chair and bounded across the room to the door to the control center. He grasped the knob, twisted it hard, then twisted it again.

"It . . . it's locked!" He stared at the others, his eyes wide with alarm. "It's locked from the other side. That *can't* be!"

Frank came to his side, jerked the knob

55

then pounded his fist against the door. "Dr. Carter," he snapped, "is there another way out of here?"

"No. Only through the control room."

"Frank," Suzanne cried out, "look at Joe's face. He's taking ten Gs, and the numbers are still climbing!"

6 Assault at Midnight

"Chet," Frank snapped, "give me a hand, quick!"

Chet was already there. "Doctor, stand aside," he shouted. Carter backed off. Frank kicked the door hard three times. Chet helped, and the two kicked together.

"No use," Frank said sharply. "It's too heavy. Let's get our backs into it."

"Hurry!" Dr. Carter gasped, positioning himself to join them. "Joe's taking eleven Gs, climbing fast to twelve. We've *got* to get him out of there!"

Frank, Chet, and Dr. Carter backed off, then threw themselves at the door. They heard wood splinter but the door wouldn't give.

"Again!" Frank shouted. The trio hurled

57

themselves forward with all the strength they could muster. The lock snapped, sounding like a gunshot. Frank and Chet went sprawling onto the floor of the control room. Dr. Carter caught himself, bounded past them, and raced for the console. A man in a grotesque Halloween mask stepped out of nowhere, spread his legs to block Carter's way and jammed a silver tube in his face. The tube hissed, and Dr. Carter fell limply to the floor!

Chet came to his feet, grabbed the assailant's legs and pulled him down. The man twisted deftly out of Chet's grip, lashed out savagely with his foot, and sent Chet sprawling. Then he ran out the door. Chet pulled himself erect, shook his head and raced after the fleeing figure.

Leaving the man in the mask to Chet Morton, Frank picked himself up and stumbled to the console board. One technician was on the floor, the other was slumped forward in his chair. Frank stared in dismay at the unfamiliar controls. The digital display blinked rapidly across the screen: *12.6 Gs . . . 13.2 . . . 14.1*—The centrifuge whirled past rapidly outside the thick window. Dr. Carter was unconscious.

Having no idea how to operate the console, Frank ignored it completely and went to his knees, tearing aside the metal panel below the board. A bewildering array of power cables and circuits met his eyes. Frank began ripping out everything in sight. White light sparked as circuits blew. The acrid smell of a dozen electrical fires burned his nostrils.

"Frank, it's stopping," Suzanne cried out. "You've done it!" She was already through the door to the centrifuge chamber, racing for the capsule.

Frank came to his feet and wiped his arm across his face. He joined her quickly and jerked open the hatch. A ragged cry escaped his throat as he saw his brother slumped limply in his straps.

"Joe, Joe, are you all right?" he cried as he tore the restraints away and held Joe's head between his hands. Joe's skin was chalk-white. Perspiration covered his face.

"Joe, come *on!*" Frank begged.

"Huh? Whassat?" Joe opened his eyes and stared up blankly at Frank. "Boy, that was a lot rougher than I thought it would be," he said hoarsely. "My eyes hurt, my chest hurts. Everything hurts!"

"I'm not a bit surprised, old buddy." Frank exchanged a weary grin with Suzanne. "Just sit still, Joe. We'll have you out of here in a minute."

He turned as Chet Morton ran into the centrifuge room, two NASA security guards on his heels. "I lost him," the chubby boy reported glumly. "He was too fast for me."

"Frank?" Joe spoke up.

"Yeah, Joe, what?"

"Did I pass the test all right? I sure hope so. I don't think I want to do it again."

Frank gripped his brother's shoulder. "Joe," he said solemnly, "You *more* than passed it. You deserve a medal for what you've just been through." While Joe regained his strength, Frank explained what had happened in the centrifuge chamber and the control room.

Suzanne Stone looked thoughtfully past the back of the house toward the beach. The surf was high, and Joe and Chet were meeting the waves head on. With them were two of Suzanne's friends, Marion Healy and Jean Blackwell.

Mr. Hardy had left a hastily written note telling the boys he'd flown to Las Vegas. A plane belonging to Consolidated Express, one of the many companies offering coast-to-coast delivery of packages, had been hijacked by a lone gunman. The plane had been ordered to land in the Nevada desert. The pilot and copilot were blindfolded and bound in the cabin. When they had managed to work themselves free, the hijackers were gone, along with all the cargo. Police found the tracks of a small truck that had pulled up beside the plane's cargo hatch. Authorities felt there was a definite link between the hijacking and Mr. Hardy's case.

"Maybe Dad's got a break this time," Frank told Suzanne. "All the other crimes were committed with no apparent motive. It's clear the crooks were after something in this case, though."

"If they took everything off that plane," Suzanne mused, "that probably means they were looking for something in those other cases as well. The chemical company fire, the research lab—"

"Could be," Frank answered. "But Dad's suspected all along that all of those crimes may have been committed to cover up another crime. The crooks must have wanted something being sent on that plane. It was easier to haul away the entire cargo than to stick around searching for the package they wanted."

"And maybe get caught in the act," Suzanne finished. A shadow suddenly crossed her features. "*My* dad could use a little help on his case," she sighed. "Unless it's already too late." She turned to face Frank, and he read the deep concern in her eyes. "That centrifuge business was the last straw. The man who tried to kill Joe got away without a trace. Dad's talking about resigning. He doesn't want Maxwell Grant to have to let him go. They're too close for that."

"There are thousands of people working at NASA," Frank protested. "Your father and his men can't watch everyone who works there every minute."

"I know," Suzanne agreed, "but if something goes wrong, he's responsible. That's the way it is."

"We'll get them," Frank said firmly. "Those characters are taking too many chances. They'll trip themselves up soon. Hey, look," he grinned, trying to take Suzanne's mind off her troubles, "I'd say 'Super G' Joe Hardy's feeling fine. I wonder if your friend Marion has anything to do with that. She's sure a good-looking girl."

"You just forget about Marion Healy," Suzanne said with half a grin.

"Who, me?" Frank blinked with no expression at all. "Why, I barely noticed her."

Suzanne punched him lightly on the arm,

and they both laughed and walked down to meet the four returning from the beach.

By the time the others had changed from swimsuits back to jeans, Suzanne and Frank had steaks sizzling on the backyard barbecue. Music thundered through the open door from the big stereo speakers inside. After the excitement of the day, the boys were relaxed and enjoying themselves immensely. Still, the Hardys and Chet Morton knew better than to leave themselves open to further danger. Utilizing the sophisticated equipment in their van, they had rigged up an electronic alarm system that would warn them if anyone approached within two hundred yards of the house. They'd been warned more than once, and didn't intend to risk their lives through carelessness.

Late in the evening, when Suzanne and her two friends were talking in a corner, Chet drew Frank and Joe aside. "I thought you guys ought to see this," he said handing them a photograph. "I don't know what good it'll do, but—well, here it is."

Frank and Joe took the 8 by 10 print and held it under the light in the hall. It showed a man running, frozen in midstride. He wore a Halloween mask.

"Hey," Frank exclaimed, "it's the man that gassed the technicians and Dr. Carter, right?"

"That's him," Chet said. "When I saw I couldn't catch him, I pulled out my mini-camera and just pointed it in his direction. I really didn't expect to get a thing."

"That's a pretty good blowup, considering the size of the film you were using," Joe said. "Don't knock it, Chet. He may have worn a mask, but now we have a record of his body size and physical characteristics. We can come pretty close to calculating his height and weight from this. It's a start."

"I don't know," Chet muttered. "He isn't fat, thin, short, or tall. If there's anything I hate it's an average crook. Probably matches over half the men working at NASA."

"Well, at least we don't have to worry about the other half," Frank grinned.

"Hey, what are you guys up to?" Marion Healy called out. "Joe, you promised to tell me how you solved your last case."

Frank chuckled. "*Your* last case, huh? I seem to remember Chet and I were around somewhere too."

Joe turned a brilliant shade of red. "Yeah, well . . . you both . . . really helped out a lot."

Chet and Frank exploded with laughter, and this time the girls joined in. Besides the name "Super G," Joe was now stuck with "Sherlock Hardy" for the rest of the evening.

Marion and Jean drove back to town at eleven. Frank planned to take Suzanne home in the rental car Mr. Hardy had left behind.

"Get a good night's sleep," Joe warned Suzanne. "We have more NASA testing to-morrow."

"Maybe we'll try out weightlessness in the underwater tank," Chet put in.

"That sounds fine to me," Suzanne said evenly. "I'd rather try weightlessness than gravity. I imagine you'd agree, Joe."

"*I'm* finished with the G business," Joe pointed out. "It's *you* characters that have to try it yet." He shot his brother a grin. "If they ever get that console put back together, that is. Frank did a pretty good job of tearing it apart."

"You'd better be glad I did, pal," Frank told him. "Suzanne, are you ready?"

"If you're sure I can't stay and help clean up."

"Joe and Chet wouldn't hear of it," Frank said firmly. "They love to clean up."

"Your share will be right here when you get back," Chet reminded him.

Frank and Suzanne started for the door, then stopped as the phone rang shrilly in the hall.

"Probably Dad, wondering what's happened to me," Suzanne said.

Joe picked up the receiver and said hello. Then he listened and the grin on his face disappeared. "Wait," he snapped, "don't hang up. Who *is* this?" He set down the phone and faced the others. "Someone wants to meet us on the beach about three miles south of here at midnight. He says he has information about the people who tried to kill me today."

"And he didn't give his name, right?" Frank asked.

"Nope. He said he was a friend."

"Hah!" Chet made a face. "I'll bet. Does he think we're crazy? That call is spelled T-R-A-P *Trap.*"

"You're right, of course," Frank said. "It's almost certain to be just that." He looked thoughtfully at the others. "Okay, what do you want to do?"

Chet let out a sigh and looked at the ceiling. "I guess we'll have to go and find out—what else?"

7 Hot Wheels

For twenty minutes, Joe had been lying flat atop the roof of the van, scanning the beach with his night vision scope while Frank drove along the lonely stretch of road. Suzanne sat with Frank, ready to man the powerful spot. Chet was stationed behind the van's command console, monitoring the array of SAT (Search and Target) gear. The mysterious caller had suggested a meeting place some three hundred yards below the sandy road. The Hardys had no intention of going anywhere near the place until they were certain they weren't driving into a trap.

"You spot anything?" Frank spoke quietly into his mike. "Anything at all?"

"Nothing," Joe answered. "A couple of people walking on the beach, that's all. If anyone's waiting for us, they're doing a good job of keeping out of sight."

"That's just what they would do," Chet said darkly.

"I'll drive to the cutoff and turn back," Frank said. "We'll try another run to make sure. It's almost 12:30. If our enemies are coming, they're late."

"If it's a trap they're not late; they just got here before we did," Joe told him. "Where they could be hiding, though, I'm not really . . . hey, Frank, hold it!" he said suddenly. "There's a car up ahead, pulled over alongside the road. It wasn't there when we passed here a minute ago."

"I see it," Frank said, braking the van to a stop.

"You've got a live one," Chet reported. "The beeper-tracker shows one warm body, driver's side. Uh-oh, he's moving. Got him, Joe?"

"Got him," Joe snapped. "He's out of the car, coming this way." Joe set the nightscope aside and peered into the dark. The man stopped twenty yards from the van.

"Frank, Joe?" a voice called out softly. "It's me, Lew Gorman."

"Mr. Gorman?" Joe blinked in surprise. "What—what are *you* doing out here?"

Harry Stone's security aide chuckled in the dark. "I was about to ask you guys the same thing."

Joe climbed down the side of the van. Frank and Suzanne were already approaching Gorman.

"I saw the van and figured it was yours," Gorman said. He glanced curiously at Frank. "Don't tell me. You got a phone call, right?"

"Did you?" Frank said cautiously. "Is that what you're saying?"

Gorman grinned. "You fellows don't trust anyone, do you? Well, I don't blame you. Yeah, I got a call. A man said to meet him here at midnight. He also said he'd tell me the name of the foreign agent working at NASA."

"We got the same call," Frank admitted. "It has to be a trap, or a very unfunny joke. I—"

"Frank, what's that?" Suzanne said suddenly. She cocked her head and listened.

"I hear it," Joe said. "It sounds like a car. But the highway's not that close."

"Sound carries farther than you think," Gorman said. "Sometimes it's a—"

"Frank, Joe!" Chet stuck his head out of the side of the van. "I've got a blip coming in fast over the dunes. Portside twenty degrees!"

Frank whirled around to his left. For an instant, he froze in a half crouch. The high-

69

pitched sound of a souped-up engine ripped through the night. A split second later, bright headlights stabbed the night.

"Take cover, everyone," Frank blurted. "Hurry!"

Lew Gorman started for his car, changed his mind and leaped for the safety of the van. The dark vehicle roared over the top of a dune, hung in midair, then bounced onto the road. Joe rolled to cover as a machine gun chattered in his direction. Yellow fire blossomed in the dark. Lead stitched the sand at Joe's heels and peppered the far side of the van. Gorman muttered under his breath, jerked a snub-nosed Colt .38 from under his jacket and fired three rounds at the retreating car.

"He's coming back," Joe yelled. "Get inside!" He dived into the van as the car skidded on the sand, then turned for a second run. Frank slipped past the others and sprawled into the driver's seat. The car raced by, spitting fire. Frank caught the vehicle with his lights as it vanished in a cloud of dust. It was visible for only an instant, but he saw that it was a dune buggy, rigged out with armor plating. The gunner sat in the passenger's seat with an automatic weapon.

"Okay, friend," Frank muttered between his teeth. "You want to play games, let's see how you like *this!*"

He turned the key in the ignition and the supercharged engine thundered to life. Sand whined under the wheels as the van took off with a sudden surge of power. Far down the road, the dune buggy's lights swept around in a circle. Frank gripped the wheel and jammed the accelerator to the floor.

"Frank!" Joe grabbed his brother's shoulder. "What are you doing?"

"Giving those characters something to think about," Frank said tightly. "They're coming back again. Only this time we're not sitting still!"

The oncoming lights flared in the windshield of the van. Frank hurled the heavy vehicle down the road on a collision course. The dune buggy came straight for him.

"Frank, they're not stopping!" Joe said hoarsely.

Frank didn't answer. His features were grim in the glare of the oncoming lights. Thirty yards . . . twenty. . . . Suddenly their attacker swerved off the road and tore through the dunes like a missile. Frank braked sharply, skidding the rear tires in a full half circle.

71

Then he jumped out of the van, raced to the back, and yanked the door open. The others followed.

"This van can go just about anywhere," Frank said harshly. "But we'll never make it in soft sand."

"The dirt bikes, right?" Joe asked.

"Right!" His brother turned swiftly to his friends. "Chet, plug us in and monitor, okay? And call the police. We'll try to keep those crooks busy until you get help. Mr. Gorman, will you stay with the van? You've got a weapon. If we miss these guys and they come back—"

"Got you," Gorman nodded.

"You're not leaving *me* here," Suzanne said fiercely.

"We only have two bikes," Frank told her.

"Yes, but you've got an extra helmet—and I grew up on dirt bikes, buddy."

"Come on, then," Frank grinned. "We're wasting time."

Joe had already lowered the ramp and rolled his bike onto the road. A special weapons belt was hooked to the handlebars. He removed the belt and buckled it quickly around his waist. Frank brought his bike to the ground; Suzanne hopped on behind and gripped his waist. They all put on black helmets that looked like the armored shells of beetles.

"Mike check," Joe called out, dropping the plastic visor over his face.

"I read you," Frank answered.

"Check," Suzanne echoed.

"A-okay," Chet told them from his console. "I've got the bandit at thirty degrees, heading south down the beach and running fast."

"Let's get him," Frank said, and kicked his bike to life. The two dark machines howled down the sandy road. Frank swerved to the left and swept over a dune into the air. Joe followed close behind, and the bikes hit the ground running.

"They're too far ahead," Suzanne yelled into her mike. "We'll never catch 'em now!"

"Hang on and watch," Frank told her. They left the dunes behind and raced onto the smooth sand of the beach. "Joe, hit it on one, okay? Three . . . two . . . now!"

Suzanne caught her breath as the dirt bike's scream suddenly deepened into an ear-splitting roar. The tires scarcely seemed to touch the ground as the cycle leaped forward with an incredible burst of speed.

"Wh–what have you got *under* this thing?" Suzanne gasped.

73

"Turbo-assist jets," Frank told her. "A power pack of speed when you need it." The turbos suddenly died, but the boosters had done their job.

"We're closing," Joe spoke into his mike. "I can see their lights now." He raced into the lead, crossed ahead of Frank, and took the flank nearest to the water.

"They see you," Chet reported. "Blip's moving off to starboard. Looks as if he's making a run for the road. "I—no, wait!" Chet's voice turned cold as ice. "Frank, veer off. He's not running, he's coming straight at you!"

"The guy's crazy," Joe muttered. "He must know the police are on their way."

"Crazy or not, he's still got that machine gun," Frank said darkly. "Split left, Joe. I'll take the right. Just keep him busy until the cavalry arrives!"

At once, Joe peeled off to the left, skimming the edge of the incoming tide. Frank circled wide, heading straight for the dunes. The fast, armored vehicle had to pick a target and chose Frank.

"Coming at you," Chet warned.

"Got him," Frank answered. He counted off the seconds in his head, letting the glaring lights loom closer. Suddenly, he cut the bike sharply to the right, tossing a high plume of sand in his wake, and darted in the opposite direction. The automatic weapon stitched thirty yards of sand, but Frank was already gone. The dune buggy's driver realized his mistake, turned quickly and streaked after Frank again. Frank glanced over his shoulder, saw the glare of lights behind him, and sent the bike howling down the beach at top speed.

"You're losing him," Suzanne cried out. "He's falling back."

"Where's Joe?"

"Right here," Joe replied, "to your left and straight ahead. Take off right. I'll do a crossover and pull him away."

"Good," Frank said, "just don't try anything tricky. You can't outrace those bullets. All you'll get is a—Suzanne, hang on!" he warned suddenly.

A jagged stump of driftwood loomed up out of nowhere. Frank jerked the bike aside but the motion was too fast, too sudden. He felt the cycle going and heard Suzanne scream as she fell away. He leaped free, covered his head and rolled to ease the blow. The bike tumbled crazily up ahead, spinning over the sand.

75

"Suzanne!" Frank came shakily to his knees. "Suzanne, *answer* me!"

He saw her, then, and a chill touched the back of his neck. She lay in a dark heap on the sand. The dune buggy's lights suddenly shifted, pinning her in its beam, and Frank knew the criminals had seen her, too!

8 Friend or Traitor?

"Frank, no!" Joe stared in horror as his brother's bike spun end over end through the air. He saw Suzanne hit the ground hard. A split second later, Frank leaped free, rolled and came to his knees.

Joe didn't hesitate an instant. His tires skidded precariously on the sand as he wrenched his bike in a tight circle, heading straight for the dune buggy's blinding white lights. The machine gun chattered, digging wet sand in Joe's path. He gritted his teeth and squeezed the last ounce of power from his engine. The dune buggy streaked for Suzanne, determined to run her down.

Joe's heart sank. *It's too far, I'll never make it!* He could already see it—seconds before he'd reach the girl, the dune buggy would hit her. She'd never have a chance.

Out of the corner of his eye, he saw Frank running desperately toward Suzanne's still form. He groped for the special weapons belt at his waist; his fingers grasped a heavy silver ball, slightly larger than a lemon. In one smooth motion, he pulled the release pin with his teeth, then hurled the ball straight ahead with all his strength.

Joe squeezed his eyes shut an instant before the sun grenade bounced, then exploded to the dune buggy's right. The bomb burst with an awesome blossom of light, turning night into day for a full two seconds. The vehicle swerved but kept coming. Joe's second grenade was already arcing through the air. This time, it exploded on target, directly in the dune buggy's path. The driver threw up a hand before his eyes and jerked the wheel frantically to the left. The dune buggy kicked up sand and plowed straight into the water.

Joe braked to a stop beside Suzanne. Frank reached her side an instant later.

"Get her out of here!" Joe shouted. "Head for the dunes."

Frank nodded. Without a word, he lifted Suzanne in his arms and sprinted for cover. Joe sprayed sand in a racing start and circled away from the water. The two gunmen were struggling ashore through the surf. When they reached the beach, they broke into a run, heading south into the night. The man with the automatic weapon fired several wild bursts at Joe, then gave up the effort and fled. Joe heard sirens behind him, braked the bike and saw red and blue lights flashing far down the beach.

"All right!" He grinned. "We got 'em!"

Suddenly, another sound made him turn around. He looked up, startled, as the dark shadow of a helicopter hovered over the beach to the south.

"No!" Joe pounded his handlebars in helpless rage. "No, they *can't* get away now!"

The helicopter's rotors sang with power, then the craft rose rapidly into the sky, the two assailants safely aboard. Too late, the police car rushed down the beach, lights flashing and sirens wailing. There was nothing to see now except an empty stretch of sand, and the deserted dune buggy bobbing against the waves. Joe turned away in disgust and headed toward the road.

When he got back to the others, Suzanne was sitting in the van, a cold cloth pressed against her head.

79

"She's okay," Frank told Joe. "Just got the breath knocked out of her."

"She's lucky she's still alive," Joe said grimly.

"I heard that," Suzanne snapped. "Hey, you guys, I'm going to be sore a couple of days, that's all!"

Frank stared solemnly down the beach through the open door. "I can't believe they got away by chopper," he said ruefully. "Joe, one of these days those characters are going to run out of luck!"

"Maybe." Joe glanced up the road. Lew Gorman was standing atop a dune, waiting for the police to return from the empty beach.

"I put in a call to Mr. Stone," Frank told Joe. "He's going to meet us back at the house."

"You tell him about Suzanne?"

"No. She didn't want me to. She'd rather let him see she's all right first. Joe, that was too close. If you hadn't thought of those sun grenades when you did—"

"Frank, Joe!" Chet Morton walked rapidly toward them. Both Hardys could see the grim expression on his face.

"Hey, Chet," Joe asked, "what's wrong?"

"Plenty," Chet said darkly, then glanced

over his shoulder at Lew Gorman, who still stood some distance away. "I found this," he said, pulling a thick brown envelope from under his shirt. "I was searching for a flash so I could get a look at that dune buggy's tracks. When I opened Mr. Gorman's car door, this fell to the ground."

Joe turned the envelope over curiously, then opened the flap. "Hey, that's . . . that's money!" he gasped. "A lot of money, too!"

"Five thousand dollars, to be exact," Chet said. He looked narrowly at Frank and Joe. "Now why would a man be carrying that kind of money on the seat of his car?"

"He wouldn't," Frank answered, the words turning dry in his mouth. "Not unless he planned to give it to someone, or someone had just given it to him."

Half an hour later, the group was back at the beach house, talking to Harry Stone.

"This is ridiculous," Lew Gorman flared. "Harry, I never *saw* that money before. I swear it!"

Harry Stone rubbed his chin thoughtfully and turned on his heels to face his young aide. "Lew, I believe you," he said. "I don't think for a minute that you took a payoff. What *I* think doesn't much matter though, does it?

Max Grant's got to know what happened. I can't very well keep it from him. You know how it's going to look."

"Yeah, I know all right." Gorman gripped the arms of his chair, staring out the window. Then he looked right at Stone. "I know why someone tried to frame me," he said, "and you do too, Harry. Putting that money in my car makes it look as if I'm working with the foreign agents." He forced a bitter laugh. "The number two man at NASA security! Great, huh? Boy, Nat Cramer and Pete McConnel will eat this up!"

"McConnel and Cramer don't have to know," Stone said shortly. "It's none of their business, and Max Grant won't tell them."

"He won't have to," Gorman said. letting his hands fall limply to his sides. "McConnel's got eyes everywhere. What I hate the most about this is how it makes *you* look, Harry."

"Don't worry about me right now," Stone told him.

"Mr. Gorman," Frank asked curiously, "do you have any idea how someone could have planted that money in your car?"

"Sure I do," Gorman replied. "Easiest thing in the world. My car was open in front of my house. I got the call you did and rushed out to the beach."

"And someone dropped the envelope in your front seat just before you left."

"Right. It had to happen that way."

Frank looked at the floor. "The idea, then, was to make us think you were behind those calls, that you led us to the beach so the agents could do us in, and got your payoff before we arrived."

Gorman looked curiously at Frank. "You're leading up to something. Exactly what is it?"

"Just this," Frank said. "Chet found that envelope strictly by accident. No one trying to frame you would ever imagine it would happen that way. And why try to frame you, if you were supposed to be a victim too, as you claim? What's the sense in implicating someone you're going to kill? I just don't get it, Mr. Gorman. The only person ever likely to see that money was you!"

Lew Gorman went pale, then his eyes flashed with anger. "You think I'm guilty, don't you!" he exploded.

"I didn't say that."

"Listen, buddy, if I'd found that money myself, I would have turned it over to Harry at once!"

"Lew, Frank's right," Mr. Stone said wearily. "*I* think that's what you'd do, but who else is going to believe a story like that?"

Gorman stared at his boss. It was a question he clearly couldn't answer.

The Hardys didn't hear from Mr. Stone again until late the next afternoon. Their day was filled with further tests, and orientation courses at NASA. Frank, Chet, and Suzanne tried out the repaired centrifuge, while Joe stood back and watched. Later, they toured a detailed mock-up of the shuttle itself, learning the various areas of operation, including flight control, space experiment facilities, exercise procedures, and sleeping arrangements—and how to eat and drink in space.

Back at their van that evening, they discovered Harry Stone had left them copies of a single fingerprint lifted from the dash of the abandoned dune buggy. His note informed them that NASA security and the police had a tentative identification, but no positive confirmation.

"They'll pin that guy down soon enough," Joe said, "but I'd like some answers now. How about you?"

Frank and Chet agreed. Using the van's sophisticated computer, they fed the fingerprint directly into their linkup system with such agencies as the FBI, the Central Intelligence Agency, and Interpol. Half an hour later, an image appeared on their screen. Frank made several copies, and passed the picture around. The man had dark hair, deep set eyes, hollow cheeks, and a mouth like the slash of a scar.

"Franz Wilhelm Schacht," Chet read aloud. "He's got a record a mile long and a couple of dozen aliases. Confirmed implication in terrorist activities in West Germany, the Middle East, and Central America. Every security agency in the world would like to get their hands on this guy. It says here he's been out of circulation, probably in hiding, for over two years."

"Well, he's not in hiding now," Frank said tightly. He slapped the picture with his hand. "If this is one of the characters we've been coming up against, how come he's running loose inside of NASA? Franz Schacht is wanted all over the world. He wouldn't dare show his face in public, especially in a high-level security installation!"

"I don't like to say this," Joe said grimly. "but maybe Pete McConnel's right. Maybe Mr. Stone isn't handling NASA security the way he should!"

9 Free Fall Fever

The next morning, Frank met Suzanne at the space shuttle runway.

"Maxwell Grant was waiting for Dad when we got home in the early morning hours," she said. "It was really awful, Frank. They're close friends, and Mr. Grant was trying to be so . . . so nice to Dad while he told him he'd have to give up his job as head of NASA security."

"But nothing's been proven against Lew Gorman," Frank protested. "No one has any real evidence to connect him to foreign agents."

Suzanne shook her head and stared at the long, flat expanse of runway shimmering under the hot Florida sky. Over her shoulder was the towering Vehicle Assembly Building.

Clustered about the giant structure were dozens of smaller buildings, all vital to the launch and recovery of the space shuttles.

"Mr. Grant didn't even know about last night's incident with Lew Gorman," Suzanne explained, "not until we told him what had happened. He was pretty upset, but he had already decided he had to let Dad go."

"It was that business at the centrifuge, wasn't it?" Frank said.

"You might say the centrifuge was the last straw." Suzanne made a face. "Mr. Grant called it 'an unacceptable penetration of security.' Dad's going to stay on until Mr. Grant can find a replacement, but he won't have much authority to do anything."

"I saw Pete McConnel and Nat Cramer at the administration building this morning," Frank told her. "I thought McConnel looked especially cheery. I'm sorry, Suzanne. I really am."

"I know. It's okay." Suzanne forced a smile. "Hey, come on, let's get going. We're holding up the U.S. Air Force!"

Chet and Joe were waiting under the wing of the big C-135 cargo plane, talking to a tall Air Force major. Like Frank and Suzanne, they wore standard NASA flight suits and

87

carried their helmets under their arms. As the newcomers approached, the officer turned and grinned.

"I'm Major Jack Brewster," he said. "I'll be going with you on your weightlessness familiarization flight." Brewster had a hawklike nose, a neatly trimmed mustache, and deeply tanned features. His eyes were hidden behind green-tinted sunglasses. "It's quieter down here," he went on, "so I'll explain a few things before we get airborne. This is really a two-phase operation. You'll experience the first phase with me. The second will take place this afternoon in the underwater lab. Now—" Brewster nodded toward the plane. "What happens up there is this. Weightlessness is simply the lack of gravity's force. We simulate deep space conditions by diving at a forty-five degree angle to gain speed, then pushing the plane over into a parabolic curve, an outside loop. During a fifteen to twenty second period of that loop, you'll experience weightlessness. Any questions so far?"

"I have plenty of questions," Chet told him, "but I don't *know* enough to ask a one."

Major Brewster grinned. "You will. Come on, let's get this bird upstairs."

"Okay," the officer's voice crackled in their

88

helmet receivers, "if you're ready, give me a hand signal. Fine—here we go. Captain McCall, take us into our dive."

"Commencing operation, major. Good luck back there."

The Hardys, Chet Morton, and Suzanne clung to a network of webbing on the starboard bulkhead of the plane. The test area was well padded, and all four of the *Skyfire* shuttle candidates were tethered with safety lines.

"Here we go!" Frank called out.

As the plane began to dive, he felt the strong pressure of centrifugal force pressing him against the webbing. He looked at Joe and Chet and caught them grinning with anticipation.

"Steady—" the pilot called out, "approaching Position Blue . . . *now!*"

Suddenly, Frank felt strangely disoriented, as if he'd forgotten which way was up or down. The force that had held him back disappeared. He was startled to find he was a good six inches away from the bulkhead, floating free with no support at all!

"Hey, we did it!" he laughed, "we're in free fall!"

"No kidding," Chet's voice spoke inside his helmet. "What makes you think so, Frank?"

Frank turned in time to see Chet float by. He was grinning from ear to ear, turning a lazy somersault in midair. Joe glided out of his way; Suzanne bent her knees and pushed off from the port bulkhead, drifting up to Frank.

"Great, isn't it?" she grinned. "I love it!"

"I think I could learn to like living in space," Frank said. "It's a—hey, what are you doing?"

"Bye-bye, Frank!" Suzanne braced herself on a bulkhead, pressed a finger against Frank's chest, and sent him sailing away. She laughed as he flailed his arms about helplessly, finally bouncing gently off the far wall.

"Okay," Major Brewster spoke into his mike, "we're climbing up the other end of our dive. Secure yourselves back into position."

"That was terrific," Chet said. "Do we get to do it again?"

"I don't know." Major Brewster gave him a long, serious look. "Do you have another quarter?"

"Huh?" For an instant, Chet's jaw fell in disappointment. Then, he saw Joe trying to keep from laughing and blushed a bright shade of red.

"Don't feel bad." The major grinned. "It works every time. Everyone from corporal to general falls for it. Captain McCall, let's take her around for a couple of more runs. We've got some satisfied customers back here."

Later that afternoon, Frank Hardy felt a peculiar sense of disorientation, a quick moment of panic when he was totally unsure of where he was. Taking a deep breath, he turned carefully in the water. He'd learned, in the plane, and again when they had first entered the underwater tank, that without the restraining force of gravity, a sudden motion could send you hurtling out of control.

Now, he asked himself calmly, *where is it? Which is the bottom of the tank and which is the top?*

The water faded to a deep, turquoise blue in both directions—fifty feet up, fifty feet down. Frank knew the NASA facility had been constructed deliberately to confuse the candidates being tested. Learning to know exactly where you were was vitally important to living in space.

Okay, Frank decided, that way is definitely up. There were two orange stripes on the curved section of piping nearby. The broader band had been on top when he'd descended. It was still there, which told him he was right side up.

"Frank, Chet," Dr. Bill O'Hara's voice

came through the earphones, "we're going to test your ability to perform tasks under weightless conditions now. Meet Suzanne and Joe at the yellow level."

"Roger, control," Frank answered. He moved cautiously to his right, trailing his oxygen line behind him. It felt like crawling through syrup. Each of them had weights attached to their "space" suits, carefully balanced to keep them suspended within their watery environment. Dr. O'Hara had explained they were neutrally buoyant, weighing exactly as much as the water they displaced. As long as they didn't move, they would neither sink nor rise to the surface. This was much like the condition they would encounter in space, away from the gravitational pull of the Earth.

Frank saw Chet to his right, and pointed straight ahead. Chet nodded and followed. They made their way through a maze of curved walls fading away in every direction. Colored lights blinked on and off all around them. It was hard to tell just where the walls led, or how far away the lights might be. It was all part of the plan to help them learn how to determine distance and direction without the help of gravity.

Two bulky white suits appeared in the

distance, and the boys recognized Joe and Suzanne.

"You'll see two red metal bars bolted to that scaffolding nearby," Dr. O'Hara instructed from above. "There will also be wrenches and two blue bars. You'll work in your present teams, and do the following: bolt the blue bars exactly eight feet below, and parallel to the red bars. You aren't allowed to use your hands or bodies to measure and you're not to float off and judge your work from a distance. You have to 'eyeball' this one—get as close as you can within the rules. Any questions?"

"Is there a time limit?" Suzanne asked.

"All I can say is your score will be evaluated on the basis of both accuracy and speed. I'm restricting communications now. You'll be able to talk only with your own team member. Anything else? All right, begin!"

Frank picked up their metal bar while Chet retrieved the wrench. Almost at once, they learned it wasn't easy maneuvering the extra weight.

"Hold the wrench and the bar against the scaffolding," Frank suggested. "That way, their weight won't affect us."

"Good idea," Chet replied. He studied the red bar bolted above. "You know what? I've got an idea this isn't as easy as it looks."

93

"I'm afraid you're right. That red bar isn't bolted on straight. At least, I don't think it is."

Chet laughed aloud. "Frank, nothing down here is straight, the bar or the scaffolding. They've got us putting together an optical illusion."

"You've hit it right on the nose," Frank said. He frowned at the scaffolding a long moment. "I think, ah, this is about the right distance, if those angles go off the way they seem from here. What do you think?"

"It's flat up there. Uh, I mean it's flatter than it's round."

"What? I don't get you, Chet."

"Sure you do. I think." Chet chuckled to himself. "I *think* that's what I think you think."

Frank turned and brought his faceplate close to Chet's. "You okay, buddy?"

"Sure I am!"

"All right," Frank said irritably. "Come on, let's get at it."

"At it . . . at it . . . *add* it. Minus two and carry your blue." Chet stuck out his tongue at Frank.

"Knock it off," Frank snapped. "We've got to get a decent score on this."

"Oh sure, get a score." Chet raised his

wrench and poked it in Frank's chest. "Don't yell at me again, Frank. I don't like it."

"Hey, what's the matter with you?" Frank backed off as Chet jabbed him hard again. The chubby boy reached out and grabbed Frank's shoulder in a strong grip.

"The fish don't like you looking at them, Frank. You think you're so smart with your little glassy window and your nice white tube with the bubbly stuff inside. You can just come and go as you please, is that what you think?"

Frank stared and pushed Chet away. "Chet, what is it? What's wrong? There aren't any fish in here and I'm not a—"

"DON'T TOUCH ME!" Chet screamed, his face twisted in anger, "DON'T EVER TOUCH ME AGAIN!"

Frank paddled frantically away in the water. Chet launched himself from the scaffolding, wrapped his legs tightly around Frank's shoulders and began tearing at the back of his helmet. Frank tried desperately to break free of the strong grip. *Chet was trying to kill him.* It didn't make sense, but there was no time to worry about that. His friend was doing his best to rip his air hose out of his suit!

10 Another Dead End

"What's happening—what's going on down there?" Dr. O'Hara's voice boomed in Frank's ears, but Frank had no time to answer. He was fighting for his life, using all the strength he could muster. He was in excellent physical condition, but Chet Morton fought like a madman. His friend struck out with savage, brutal power. It was all Frank could do to hold his own; Chet was hauling him quickly down in the depths, his arms and legs squeezing Frank's body in a viselike grip. Chet's voice screamed in his ears, a babble that made no sense at all.

"Get him off me," Frank shouted. "I need help down here—fast!"

He desperately sucked in air, then realized with sudden terror that there was no air to breathe. A stream of bubbles flashed before his faceplate. *My air hose—he's torn my air hose loose!* Frank thought.

He flailed out in sheer panic. In some small corner of his mind he knew no water would rush into his suit; a safety valve had closed the instant Chet ripped his hose away. He wouldn't drown—he'd just die of asphyxiation!

Frank gasped for breath. There was an emergency oxygen tank attached to his suit, but Chet would not let him reach it. He could see himself, now, from a great distance away. He watched his arms and legs flail out against the demon on his back. His limbs were as heavy as lead. It was too much trouble to fight back. Anyway, it didn't matter, did it? It wasn't really important—

No! Fight it, fight it! a voice called out from far away.

What for? he answered himself. *Too tired . . . got to . . . take it easy . . . get a little sleep—*

"Frank, Frank, talk to me!" Suzanne's anxious features swam before his eyes.

"Huh? Su–Suzanne?" Past her, he saw the interlaced girders of the ceiling.

"He'll be all right," a voice said behind him.

97

"Here, keep this oxygen mask handy if he needs it."

Frank took a deep breath. "I know this is a stupid question, but where am I?"

"On the floor, Frank." Suzanne forced a smile and touched his brow. "We're still in the tank room."

"The tank room . . . *Chet!*" He jerked up quickly and Suzanne eased him back.

"They've taken him to the base hospital. He'll be all right," she assured him. "We got you both out in time. Just barely, though." She closed her eyes and shook her head. "It was awful, Frank. It took Joe and me and three of the lab's divers to get him off you."

"Suzanne, what happened?" Frank asked. "Chet just went crazy all of a sudden!"

"That's exactly what he did."

Frank turned to see Harry Stone's grim features at his daughter's shoulder. "Someone slipped this little killer into the valve that connected Chet's air hose to his oxygen supply above." He held up a circular object between his fingers, a shiny disk the size of a silver dollar. "We'll have the lab confirm it, but I can tell you what they'll find. Some kind of powerful hallucinogenic crystals were placed in this disk before it was slipped into

98

Chet's valve. Moisture forming within the hose converted the crystals to gas." Stone's eyes went dark with anger. "I've seen this stuff before. If we hadn't reached Chet when we did, he might have suffered permanent damage. We came awfully close to losing both of you down there."

Frank pulled himself up and leaned against the cold wall. He saw the white suits and helmets that had been dropped hastily to the floor and looked away. "Someone doesn't want us on this case," he said wearily. He glanced around the room. "Where's Joe? Is he okay?"

"He's fine," Suzanne told him. "He went to the hospital with Chet."

"Good. Give me a hand, will you, Mr. Stone?" Frank said.

"You sure you feel like walking?"

"I feel like getting out of here," Frank said soberly. "This place is beginning to give me the creeps."

They walked down the long hall and out of the lab building. Frank blinked against the sudden harsh light of the day.

"Oh, no," Suzanne said suddenly, "not those two!"

Frank followed her glance and saw Maxwell

99

Grant striding purposefully toward the building, Nat Cramer and Pete McConnel on his heels.

"Frank, are you all right?" Grant said anxiously. "I got here as soon as I could."

"I'm fine, Mr. Grant. A little shaken up is all. Chet got the worst of it, I guess."

McConnel walked up and shook his finger in Grant's face. "How long are you going to put up with this, mister!" he snapped. "We're all in danger, as long as this—this incompetent is allowed to run NASA security!"

"You know as well as I do Harry Stone has been dismissed," Grant said stiffly. "He'll be off NASA facilities as soon as I can find a replacement."

"Oh, that's great!" McConnel gave Stone a malicious grin. "And what are we supposed to do until then? Let the foreign spies who work for Stone blow up the place?" He gave Grant a sly, knowing look. "Didn't think I knew about Gorman and his five grand payoff, did you?"

Maxwell Grant's features went hard. "McConnel, I don't need you to tell me how to run this operation."

"I have tried to be patient about this," Nat Cramer broke in. "But Pete's right. You're endangering everyone who works here, the

Skyfire shuttle, and my company's *Longeye* project."

"I understand your concern—" Grant began.

"Then get rid of this guy," McConnel bellowed. "Get rid of him now, Grant!"

Harry Stone made a noise in his throat and went for McConnel.

"Mr. Stone, no!" Frank cried out. He lunged for the security chief and pinned his arms to his waist. Grant stepped quickly in front of his friend.

"Go on, let him go," McConnel laughed. "I'll take you on any time, Stone. Any time!"

When Frank arrived back at the beach house late that afternoon, he found another surprise awaiting him in the den. Mr. Hardy sat in a large easy chair. His right leg was propped up on a stool and encased in a heavy plaster cast.

"Dad!" Frank cried. "What on earth happened to you?"

"It's a long story," Mr. Hardy grumbled. "I followed through on that Nevada hijacking, and got a lead on the man who drove the truck full of cargo away from the plane. He was hiding in the garage behind his house in Phoenix, Arizona."

He paused and gave Frank a rueful look. "Only there were two of them. I winged one, and his partner got me. Too bad, I almost had 'em! Instead, they both vanished into thin air and I'm wrapped up in this thing!"

Frank was silent a long moment. "What were they up to, Dad? What were they after?"

"I had a pretty good idea before the hijacking," Fenton Hardy told him. "I'm almost certain, now. My investigators have done some backtracking on the other cases. The chemical company, the research facility. . . . In every incident the plans for some new invention, or parts of the device itself, were supposedly destroyed when the crooks broke in."

"Industrial secrets!" Frank exclaimed.

"Right. And you can bet one of the packages stolen from that plane will bear me out."

Frank looked puzzled. "But the executive who was kidnapped—how does he fit in?"

Mr. Hardy grinned. "We've had a breakthrough there. As soon as we decided what had to be going on, we questioned the man again. He revealed that there are periods during his capture he can't recall. We have some pretty firm evidence that he was drugged. That means he fits right into the picture. His company was working on a new process, and my guess is the crooks stole that information right out of his head!"

"Then you're dealing with a gang of industrial thieves."

"And a clever, well organized gang at that." Fenton Hardy gripped the arms of his chair, then looked straight at Frank. "Seems to me things are getting a little rough around here as well, son. I had two calls before you arrived. One from Maxwell Grant, the other from Harry Stone. Between the two of them, they told me enough about what you have been going through to make my hair stand on end."

"We've had all the excitement we need," Frank agreed.

"I won't tell you to quit," Mr. Hardy said, "I know how you'd all react to that. Just be extra careful from now on."

"We'll do that for sure," Frank promised.

"Oh, I almost forgot. Max said Joe and Chet are on their way home. Chet's fine. And if you're all up to it, Max would like to treat you to dinner tonight. Sort of a celebration in honor of passing all the pre-flight tests for *Skyfire*. That's just a day and a half away."

"I know," Frank said. "What about Suzanne? Is she invited too? She's part of our shuttle group, you know."

Mr. Hardy cleared his throat. "Grant said

he asked her. Suzanne felt she ought to stay with her father."

"I don't blame her," Frank said gloomily. "Dad, they're sure giving Mr. Stone a hard time."

"I know Harry Stone pretty well. He'll come through this all right."

"I'll tell you one thing," Frank said firmly. "Pete McConnel had better stay out of his way. Mr. Stone's had about all he can take from that character!"

Half an hour later, Joe and Chet arrived. Chet saw Frank, stared at the floor and stuck out his hand.

"I'm sorry about what happened," he said. "You know I couldn't help what I was doing, Frank."

"Huh?" Frank looked puzzled. "What are you talking about, Chet? I thought you were making a lot more sense than usual."

Joe and Mr. Hardy laughed.

"If I were you I wouldn't sleep too soundly tonight," Chet said, giving Frank his best malicious grin. "I might just have a relapse!"

11 He's Been Shot!

In spite of the tempting offer of an evening at the Champs Élysées, one of the area's finest restaurants, Chet decided to stay home after his trying ordeal.

"Boy, he must really feel awful," Joe said. "I can't remember Chet ever turning down a good meal."

"I don't think it has much to do with how he feels—physically, I mean," Frank mused. "What happened in that tank scared the life out of Chet. And I don't blame him a bit. Everything I've read about the effect of hallucinogenic drugs on the mind tells me it's a terrifying experience. I was pretty scared myself, just being close to something like that."

"To say nothing about nearly getting asphyxiated," Joe added.

"Yeah, there's that," Frank said dryly. "I'm not very likely to forget."

South of the space center, a bright string of lights winked from Cocoa Beach to Patrick Air Force Base and beyond. Frank checked his directions and wheeled the van off busy Highway 1.

"There it is," he told Joe, "the Champs Élysées."

"At least it's different," Joe grinned. "Everything else you see around here, from motels to grocery stores, is named 'missile,' 'astronaut,' 'satellite,' or 'moon flight.'"

Frank found a spot in the parking lot, and they made their way toward the restaurant. The Champs Élysées, named after the most celebrated boulevard in Paris, was built in the shape of an eighteenth-century French farmhouse.

"Boy," Joe said, closing his eyes and sniffing the air, "I don't know what they're cooking in there, but I like it already."

"Just remember," Frank warned, "tell Chet the food was awful, and he didn't miss a thing."

"Don't worry." Joe laughed. "I wouldn't

106

think of— Hey, Frank, do I see who I think I see?"

"It's Mr. McConnel, all right," Frank said. "Now what's *he* doing here?"

"Maybe he heard the food was good," Joe suggested.

Pete McConnel stepped out of a car by the curb and stalked hurriedly toward them across the lot, his features set in their usual bulldog scowl. The Hardys could see Nat Cramer waiting in the driver's seat beyond.

"I'm glad I caught up with you fellows," McConnel said darkly. "You alone? Anyone with you?" His ball-bearing eyes swept furtively around the lot.

"Yes, we're alone," Frank said cautiously. "Mr. McConnel, how did you know where to find us? I'm sure Dad didn't tell you."

"That's not important," McConnel snapped. "I find out what I need to find out." Once more, he glanced nervously over his shoulder. "Look, I've got to talk to you guys. If you don't mind, let's step over there out of the light."

"What for?" Joe asked.

"Just do it, okay?" McConnel urged. The Hardys followed him into the shadow of the overhanging roof. "I know you two don't like me very much," he went on. "Forget that. I've

107

got a job to do, and I'm not trying to win a popularity contest."

"Never mind that," Frank told him. "What is it you have to say?"

"Listen and listen carefully!" the security man said tightly. "You're in danger, great danger. The people behind this thing will stop at nothing. They're determined to see that the *Skyfire* mission never gets off the ground. Anyone who stands in their way is going to end up dead."

"You're not exactly telling us anything new," Frank said wryly. "We've had more than one run-in with these characters."

McConnel's features went hard. "That's just it. You're in a lot more danger than you imagine. Because you don't know who you're up against. You've picked the wrong people to trust."

"Oh, come on now," Joe said irritably. "You're not going to start that stuff again, are you?"

"You're not listening!" McConnel blurted. His face went dark with rage, and for the first time the Hardys saw fear in the man's eyes. "I'm telling you this for your own good," he growled. "You can believe me or not, that's up to you. When you go inside, tell Maxwell Grant I have proof that th—"

The sharp crack of a pistol shot cut through the night. McConnel's face contorted in pain. He grabbed his shoulder, stumbled, and sprawled on the ground.

"Get down, get *down!*" he cried out, clawing desperately for the weapon under his jacket. Frank and Joe leaped for cover as the gunman fired again, four quick shots in a row. Lead dug at the asphalt paving. A bullet hit the restaurant wall and sprayed Joe with shards of brick.

"There he is," Frank shouted, "between those cars!"

McConnel's pistol thundered from the ground. The gunman jerked frantically aside. He stood frozen, surprised by McConnel's volley, then leaped over the hood of a car. For a split second before he disappeared, Joe saw his face caught in the parking lot's lights.

Schacht. Franz Schacht! Joe's throat went suddenly dry. It was the terrorist for certain. There was no mistaking the man's features.

"Joe, get help fast!" Frank yelled.

Joe was already on his way, sprinting for the door of the restaurant. People began to gather on the sidewalk, and he stopped the first man he saw.

"Call the police," he said firmly, "and get an ambulance out here. A man's been shot!"

The man ran quickly inside. Joe raced back around the corner, where Frank was bending over Pete McConnel. McConnel's face was pale. Blood soaked through his jacket.

"An ambulance is on the way," Joe reported. "How bad is he?"

"I'm all right," McConnel growled. He shook off Frank's help and got shakily to his feet. "I've been shot before. I'll make it okay."

Frank turned as Nat Cramer appeared at his shoulder. "Pete," he cried. "Wh–what happened!"

"We had us a little shoot-out, Nat." McConnel held his shoulder and glared at the Hardys. "You guys want to know why they tried to kill me?" he asked flatly. "Because I've got proof, that's why, proof that your good friend Lew Gorman worked for a foreign power before he came to NASA, and still does!"

"What?" Frank stared.

"You heard me, and unless I miss my guess, Harry Stone is up to his neck in this business, too!" He gave the Hardys a hollow grin and rested his good arm over Cramer's shoulder. "I'm going to get patched up," he said. "When the police get here, you tell 'em I'll be glad to drop over and give them a statement."

"We've called an ambulance," Joe said. "It'll be here soon."

McConnel laughed aloud. "If I wait around for those characters I'll probably bleed to death. Come on, Nat, get me out of here before I fall on my face."

Frank and Joe watched until Cramer burned rubber and headed for Highway 1. A crowd was gathering now, and Frank saw a familiar face push his way through.

"Frank, Joe!" Maxwell Grant's jaw fell. "What happened out here? You two weren't involved, were you?"

"It's a long story," Frank said wearily, as a wail of sirens sounded in the distance. "I don't think it's one you're going to like much, either."

It was nearly midnight before the police finished questioning Lew Gorman. In spite of the angry protests of Pete McConnel, the detectives found no reason to hold him. The problems of NASA and national security were beyond their jurisdiction. They were solely concerned with the shooting at the Champs Élysées, and Joe had definitely identified the gunman as Franz Wilhelm Schacht.

Harry Stone arrived moments after Gorman was released. Grant took Stone aside and talked with him for nearly a quarter of an hour. Then Stone joined his aide and the Hardys at a small all-night diner.

"It's all a mistake," Gorman said wearily. "I did work in security at Morgan Electronics before you hired me, Harry. Their name is on my job application." He paused and stared into his coffee. "After I got the job at NASA, a friend told me he'd learned Morgan Electronics is secretly owned by a North African nation, one that's not exactly friendly with the United States right now. I was afraid to say anything to you. I didn't want to lose my job. I sure couldn't speak up after that business on the beach. I knew you'd never believe me after that money was found in my car. I should have been straight with you, but I wasn't."

"Yes, you should have," Stone said evenly. "Not that it matters much now. We're both out of work. Max just made that pretty clear. Neither of us is welcome at NASA any more."

"There's got to be some way to clear this mess up," Frank said hopefully.

"Fat chance," Gorman said grimly. "Someone's done a good job of framing me, but I can't prove a thing." He pounded his fist on the table, rattling china and spilling his coffee.

"I'll get even with Pete McConnel if it's the last thing I ever do!"

"Someone tried to even up the score tonight," Joe said.

Gorman's eyes flared. "Maybe you think McConnel's right, huh? That I was working with this Franz Schacht!"

"Now, I didn't say that," Joe protested.

"You didn't have to," Gorman snapped. "It's pretty clear you've all got me tried, convicted, and sentenced!" He stood up abruptly and stalked out of the diner. A moment later, his car streaked down the road, spitting dust.

12 Mask of Terror

A driving summer rain swept in from the Atlantic, turning the dark highway to shimmering glass. Frank leaned intently over the wheel, guiding the van through the early morning hours.

"I guess we learned one thing, anyway," Joe said wearily. "Franz Schacht is still in the neighborhood."

"I'll say he is," Frank nodded grimly. "And he lives up to his reputation, too. No wonder every security agency in the western world wants his hide."

Joe was silent a long moment, watching the windshield wipers sweep rapidly from side to side. "Frank," he said finally, "I'm still wondering how a character like Schacht could penetrate a place like NASA. His face is well known, and his prints are on file everywhere."

"I know," Frank agreed. "And there's something we've been overlooking, too. There's more than one foreign agent mixed up in this. Remember, two men attacked us with that dune buggy. Maybe one of them was Schacht, or maybe neither of them."

"You're right," Joe frowned. "And that means it's possible the spy inside NASA isn't Schacht at all."

"Not only possible, but very likely."

"So we don't have any idea how many infiltrators are involved," Joe muttered. "The person who tried to kill me in the centrifuge, and slipped those hallucinogenic crystals in Chet's oxygen line, could be anybody. We may have a small army of agents after us, and the only one we can identify is Schacht!"

Frank shot Joe a look. "Don't forget the bunch of crooks in Dad's case, the characters who've been trying to kill him since Okefenokee."

"Yeah," Joe said gloomily. "It's getting so you can't tell the bad guys without a program."

"Which gets us back to Lew Gorman, doesn't it?" Frank said. "Either he's working with Schacht, or someone's setting him up."

"Why, though? If he is being framed, who's behind it?"

"I can make a good guess," Frank replied. "Sowing confusion and suspicion is an old trick in the espionage game."

"You mean Schacht's gang might want us to think Gorman's involved with them?"

"Right. And Pete McConnel's hatred of Harry Stone is playing right into their hands."

"*If* Lew Gorman is innocent," Joe put in.

"Yeah, and that's a big if," Frank said. He stared thoughtfully into the rain. "I have an idea, Joe. Gorman's guilt or innocence is one of the keys to this case. If we could talk to him again, maybe come up with some information that would either prove or disprove his involvement with foreign agents—"

Joe looked startled. "You don't mean now, do you?"

"Why not?"

"After what I said to him at that diner, he's not going to be anxious to see us, especially at two in the morning."

"Like Pete McConnel said," Frank grinned, "we're not trying to win a personality contest; we're trying to solve this case. Gorman ought to be getting home about now. If we turn around and take the cutoff back there, we can

116

be at his place in fifteen minutes. You apologize and I'll try to convince him we want to help. All he can do is kick us out."

"Sure," Joe said soberly, "or shoot us on sight with that Colt .38 he carries."

The rain had eased to a light drizzle by the time the Hardys found the road that led to Lew Gorman's home. He lived in one of the many new developments that had sprung up near the Intercoastal Waterway since NASA had come to Florida's eastern coast. Frank instinctively doused the van's lights as they approached Gorman's street. Just as they swung around the corner, a small Italian sports car darted out of a driveway ahead, skidded on the slick street, and vanished into the mist.

"Frank, isn't that—"

"It's Gorman's car, all right," Frank said tightly. "He's sure in a hurry to get somewhere, too."

"We'll be lucky if we don't lose him," Joe said. "Lights or no lights, he'll spot this van in a minute, especially at this time of the morning."

Frank kept his distance, letting the rain form a protective curtain between the van and the sportscar. Then he switched the super-charged motor to its special whisper cycle to mask the engine's noise.

Instead of heading to the highway, Gorman led them past the development toward a lonely stretch of beach. The Hardys could see fuzzy points of light far out in the water, buoys in the intercoastal canal.

"Uh-oh," Joe said, "fog's rolling in. He'll lose us for sure now."

"He already has," Frank said. "I can't be certain, but I think he's turned off. I don't dare go any farther in case he's stopped."

Frank pulled the van off the road. Joe grabbed a flashlight from under the dash, and the boys got out. They shut the doors silently and jogged quickly through the mist. A few minutes later, Frank touched his brother's arm lightly and pointed to the right.

"That's his car," he whispered. "Take it easy now. He has to be around here."

"What's he doing out here?" Joe said uneasily. "Frank, he could be meeting those foreign agents. Maybe even. Franz Schacht himself."

"Look, there he is," Frank said suddenly. "Get down!"

The Hardys huddled on the wet ground behind a ragged clump of sea grass. Not more than twenty yards away, a shadowy figure appeared out of the fog. Frank and Joe watched as Gorman stopped, bent his shoulders, straightened, and bent again. The slow, steady sound of a shovel striking sand reached their ears. Finally, Gorman straightened, looked carefully in every direction, then set his shovel aside and kneeled to the ground.

A wave of heavy mist rolled in from the sea and the boys could not see Gorman for a few moments. When the area was clear again, he was gone. Moments later, a car door slammed and an engine was revved up. Frank ran to the road to make certain the disappearing car was Gorman's, then joined his brother again. Joe was already at the spot where they had seen Gorman, and was digging in the sand with his hands.

"Here," he said, "hold the light. He wasn't here five minutes. He couldn't have dug very deep. Hey, I've got something!" Joe lifted a small, plastic bag out of the hole and laid it on the ground. "Now," he said firmly, "let's see what's important enough to bury at three in the morning. Whatever it is, it's got to be a—Frank, will you look at this!"

Joe caught his breath and stared at the mask in his hand. The cold light of the flash turned the limp rubber cheeks and sagging mouth stark white. Joe stuck his fingers through the empty eyeholes. Even without a face to fill it out, it was easy to see the mask was a perfect likeness of Franz Schacht!

"Well, so much for helping Lew Gorman," Frank said flatly. "I'm afraid we just put him behind bars!"

Leaden gray clouds swept low over the sky early next morning. Rain from the night before still dampened the stone steps of the somber municipal building that housed the local courthouse and police station. Joe Hardy yawned, glanced at his watch, and saw it was 6:35 A.M.

"All I have to say is it's sure been one busy night. I'm glad it's about over."

"I wish it hadn't turned out the way it did," Frank said sadly. "I'm not at all happy to find out what Lew Gorman is."

Fenton Hardy turned to face his son, leaned against the van, and eased the crutches under his arms. "Frank, there was nothing else you could do," he said firmly. "A piece of evidence like that isn't something you can ignore."

"I know, Dad. But I don't have to like it."

The Hardys glanced up as Maxwell Grant

walked out of the gray building with Chet Morton and started across the street. Frank thought Grant looked as if he'd aged a hundred years overnight.

"They're still talking to Gorman," Grant said when he reached the van. "The F.B.I.'s with him now, and a couple of men from the State Department." He shook his head in dismay. "What a nightmare, Fenton. I can't believe all this is happening!"

"Has Mr. Gorman admitted anything yet?" Joe asked.

"Not a thing," Grant said flatly. "He still claims the mask was planted in his house. When he found it, he ran out and buried it, figuring no one would believe him." Grant made a face. "He's right, too. Nobody does, and that includes me. Gorman yells 'frame up' every time you turn around. Has anyone seen Harry Stone? I thought he'd be here by now."

"We called him," Joe said, "right after we notified the police. He said he'd meet us here."

Grant glanced at his watch. "He's sure taking his time. I can't wait around any longer. I have to get over to NASA and explain to *my* boss how I managed to let a foreign agent into my security section." He nodded at Frank and Joe. "You'd better get some rest. If this weather clears up, you'll be in deep space this time tomorrow."

Joe looked at his brother. Frank's expression clearly mirrored his own thoughts. "I can't believe it's possible," he told Grant, "but with everything that's been happening around here, we almost forgot we were going!"

13 He's a Spy!

"I'm hungry," Joe said on the way back to the beach house.

Frank stared at the road. "You can eat if you like. All I want is a good soft bed." He turned to his father who was in the passenger seat with his injured leg stretched out before him.

"One thing keeps bothering me, Dad," he said thoughtfully, "though it may not matter much now. We know there's a real Franz Schacht. His prints were on that dune buggy. He was driving it while Gorman was with us."

"So why all the business with a mask that looks like Schacht?" Fenton Hardy countered. "I can't say for sure, but I can make a good guess. Deception is what spying is all about— keeping the other side off balance."

"You said it yourself, Frank," Joe reminded

123

his brother. "Confusion is the name of the game."

"If that's what they're after, then it works," Frank muttered. "I have to admit, I'm pretty confused."

"I know what you mean," Joe said. "One Franz Schacht is enough. Two is too many."

"Schacht's managed to stay in hiding for a couple of years," Frank mused. "Why would he want to call attention to himself now? Is it worth it, just to cause confusion?"

"If there's one thing I've learned in my years of police work," Mr. Hardy said, "it's that criminals usually have pretty big egos. They can't help showing off."

"Like thumbing your nose at the law, right?" Frank said.

"Exactly. I'd be willing to bet Schacht isn't all that different from your average armed robber or second-story man."

"Maybe the bigger the crook, the bigger the ego," Joe suggested.

"Wouldn't surprise me at all," Mr. Hardy said. "Schacht's been out of circulation a long time. Maybe he wants to let everyone know he's still alive and kicking, still a threat to—"

"Dad," Frank broke in, "maybe I'm just imagining things, but I think that car back there is tailing us. I've slowed a couple of times to let him pass, but he's holding back."

"Can you see anyone inside?" Joe asked.

"No, he's too far away. Besides, he's got that dark-tinted glass on his windows. Hey, wait—" Frank sat up straight and peered intently into his sideview mirror. "I'm sure of it now. He's suddenly coming up right behind us!"

Mr. Hardy glanced in his own mirror. "I don't like this at all," he said tightly. "Hold 'er steady, son. Watch your speed."

"He—he's passing," Frank exclaimed, "swerving to the left. No! He's gone again."

"Good grief, the fool's trying to pass us on the right!" Mr. Hardy cried.

Frank jammed his foot against the floor. The van shot forward with an incredible burst of speed.

"He's still coming," Mr. Hardy shouted. "He's—*Frank, get us out of here. He's got a gun!*"

Before Frank could answer, lead rattled against the side of the van. Frank jerked the wheel to the left. The screeching of rubber against asphalt reached his ears over the shatter of gunfire. The car almost scraped the van, then raced ahead, skidding dangerously

125

as the tires left the shoulder and gripped the road again. In seconds, the attacker was nearly out of sight.

"Dad, are you all right?" Frank called out, "is everyone okay?"

"We're fine back here," Joe said shakily. "We'd be mincemeat, though, if it wasn't for the van's armor plating!"

"I got the license," Frank said, "for all the good it'll do. The car's probably stolen."

"We don't need a license," Mr. Hardy said slowly. "I got a good look at the driver. He stared right at me while he pulled the trigger."

Frank caught the pain in his father's voice and turned to face him. "Dad, what's wrong? Who was it?"

"It was Harry," he said without expression. "Harry Stone is the man who just tried to kill us!"

The Hardy boys and Chet, whom they had picked up on the way, were standing in front of Harry Stone's house an hour later. The street was filled with police cars and unmarked government vehicles. Officers and security agents were swarming around the place.

"They're still questioning Stone," Pete

McConnel was saying. "He claims he didn't do it, of course. Says he was just leaving the house to join you after he learned Lew Gorman had been arrested. He came outside and found he had *two* flat tires. He got one changed and was going through his garage looking for another he could use. That's what he was doing when the police got here."

"Did anyone see him," Joe asked. "A neighbor, maybe?"

"Not likely," Frank answered. "His driveway's behind the house, back of that fence."

"What are you guys talking about?" McConnel gave the Hardys a sour look. "Of course they didn't see him. He wasn't there. Someone changed a tire for him, all right. Maybe Schacht himself, or one of Stone's other spying friends. But it wasn't Harry Stone. We know where he was. Your father's the one who turned him in, remember?"

"We remember," Frank said coolly. "We're just trying to look at the thing from all angles."

"Well, try this angle on for size," McConnel said bluntly. "They found the stolen car abandoned not five blocks from here. The Uzi submachine gun he used was still in the front seat—an M23, 9-millimeter job. It's a favorite terrorist weapon, by the way. And it's been established that he had plenty of time to ambush your van and get back here!"

Frank stared glumly at the house. His father and Maxwell Grant were inside. Frank wondered if they'd been allowed to talk to Stone. Moments before, he'd learned Suzanne was home as well. She'd been with her friend Marion Healy, but the police had sent a car to bring her back.

"It doesn't make sense," Joe told Pete McConnel. "Why would Mr. Stone take a chance like that? He knew any one of us could identify him."

"I thought you characters were investigators," McConnel sneered. "He was trying to kill you with that submachine gun. If you're dead, you're not going to identify anyone."

"I guess you're right," Chet said dismally.

"Of course I'm right." McConnel made a face as he shifted his arm in its sling. "Look," he said patiently, "I don't like Harry Stone. I've made no secret of that. But I'm not happy things turned out this way, whether you three believe me or not." He paused a moment, then went on. "I've got a job to do, you understand? This thing has driven my boss, Nat Cramer, up the wall. Do you know how long the Starglass Corporation has worked to perfect the *Longeye* radio telescope? Nine years. At a cost of *seventy-five million bucks*. We've got a lot invested in the *Skyfire* launch, and I'm the guy responsible for seeing the *Longeye* package is safely aboard when the shuttle leaves the ground."

"Nobody's blaming you for doing your job," Joe said soberly.

"Yeah? I'm not so sure about that," McConnel growled.

"Hey, look," Chet said to the Hardys, "there's your Dad and Mr. Grant."

Fenton Hardy came out of Stone's front door on his crutches, Maxwell Grant at his side. The boys noticed the grim expression on their father's face, and the dark glint in his eyes.

"Dad, ah, maybe you'd better sit in the van, okay?" Frank said anxiously.

Mr. Hardy shook his head. "I didn't believe it," he said tightly, "not even after I saw him with my own eyes. Not Harry, not a man that I've known for years." He took a deep breath to swallow his anger, and looked straight at Joe and Frank. "It's over. All of it. They found enough papers hidden in Harry's wall to convict him a hundred times over—him and Gorman. They're up to their necks in a Middle East espionage ring. They had us all fooled!"

"I'm sorry," Frank said, "I can't believe it either. It just—" He stopped as Suzanne's face suddenly appeared in a second-story window. She stared angrily at Frank a long moment, then turned away abrubtly and vanished from sight.

14 3--2--1--Lift-Off!

"Wow," Joe exclaimed, "that's the most beautiful sight I ever saw!"

"It's something, all right," Chet sighed. "When I think of all the times I've watched a shuttle launch on TV! I never even *dreamed* I'd be going up in one myself."

He stared in awe at the gleaming white spectacle of *Skyfire*. The orbiter craft was perched atop its massive propellant tank, along with the two smaller, solid-fuel booster rockets. Soon, Frank, Joe, and Chet would ascend the elevator in the launch scaffolding along with the rest of the crew and enter the stubby-winged craft that would hurl them into space.

"You guys have a great trip," Mr. Hardy said with a grin. He leaned on his crutches

131

and shook their hands. "Wish I were going with you. At least, I wouldn't have to hobble around like this in zero gravity."

"No, but you'd probably wreck the ship with that cast," Joe said wryly.

Mr. Hardy laughed. "You're right. I'd be a menace in space for sure." He turned and looked at Frank, who was standing by himself a few yards away. "I'm sorry," the detective told his older son soberly. "I know what's on your mind. I just wish it hadn't turned out this way."

"Yes, Dad," Frank said and shook his head. He frowned thoughtfully at the awesome sight above. "It's not right, though. Suzanne passed all the pre-flight tests, just like the rest of us. They shouldn't punish her for what happened."

"That's the way it works, unfortunately," Mr. Hardy replied. "The government's going to prosecute Harry Stone and Lew Gorman for treason, espionage, attempted murder, the works. Suzanne is Harry's daughter. Until this is over—"

"It's not ever going to be over for Suzanne," Frank said dismally.

"Crew alert," a voice from the loudspeaker announced. *"Four minutes until boarding."*

"Well, I guess this is it," Frank said. He

grasped his father's hand once more. "You get back on your feet soon."

"I'd better," Mr. Hardy said grimly. "I still have a case to unravel, remember? It's not going to get any easier while I sit around in a chair."

Frank looked past his father's shoulder. Shuttle Commander Major Rick Halman and the pilot, Jeff Cooper, were talking with Maxwell Grant and several other people from NASA. Beyond them were Brett Hilton, mission specialist for the *Skyfire* flight, and Nat Cramer of the Starglass Corporation. Although Cramer's official title was project specialist, Frank knew he was the most important member of the crew. Other experiments would be performed in space, but the launching of the *Longeye* radio telescope was unquestionably the main event.

"Crew alert . . . two minutes—"

"Okay, let's get going," Chet called out.

"They won't leave without us," Joe assured him.

"Why not?" Chet blinked. "They've managed to put a lot of other shuttles into space without our help."

"Sure, but that was before they knew *I* was available." Joe grinned.

"Oh, Frank—"

Frank turned and saw Maxwell Grant waving him over. When he reached the NASA official, Grant pointed to the phone on the scaffolding behind him.

"For you," he said. "Better hurry."

"Me?" Frank looked surprised, then picked up the receiver and said hello.

"It's me, Frank. Suzanne."

"Suzanne! Hey, it's great to hear your voice."

"I just want to wish you luck," she said sadly. "I'm sorry I couldn't talk to you before now. After what's happened, well, you understand."

"Sure I do, Suzanne. Listen, I wish you were here with us."

"So do I. It's so—oh, Frank! Good luck, good-bye!"

Suddenly, she was gone. Frank looked blankly at the phone, then slowly replaced the receiver.

A few moments later, everyone had boarded the shuttle, *"Ten. Nine. Eight—"*

The Hardys and Chet Morton lay back against their cushioned seats on the middle deck. They were firmly strapped in, staring straight up at the forward bulkhead. Directly above in the flight section, the commander and the pilot sat before their control panels.

Behind them were the project specialist and the mission specialist.

"*Seven. Six. Five—*"

Outside, the gantry had swung free, though a network of cables still linked the shuttle to the tower.

"*Four. Three. Two. One. Lift-off! We have ignition!*"

The shuttle's three main engines and the solid-fuel rocket boosters fired at once, generating an awesome 6.5 million pounds of thrust. Searing orange flame and white-hot gases howled into the concrete cooling pit below. *Skyfire* hesitated an instant, balanced on a column of smoke and fire, then rose toward the heavens with a thunderous roar. It climbed rapidly, its speed forcing the crew against their seats with two Gs of pressure.

After two minutes of flight, *Skyfire* was hurtling out of the atmosphere at 3,213 miles per hour. The solid-fuel boosters burned out and fell away. Six minutes later, the giant main propellant tank dropped free. Now, the shuttle was on its own. Its engines pushed the craft up to escape velocity speed, 17,500 miles per hour. With a final burst of power, *Skyfire* was in orbit, climbing toward a height of 310 miles above the Earth.

"All right, crew," Major Halman called out,

"you can stand easy down there. We're flying nice and smooth. As they say on the airlines, you're free to unfasten your safety belts and move around."

Chet looked at the Hardys and grinned, then loosed the harness at his shoulders and waist. The movement caused his body to rise slowly out of the seat.

"Hey, look, it works!" he exclaimed.

"Of course it works," Joe laughed. "What did you expect?"

Nat Cramer floated halfway through the flight deck hatch. The flight deck still seemed "above" and Cramer appeared to be "upside down," though the words had no meaning in the zero gravity environment.

"Major Halman says you're welcome to come up and have a look at Earth," Cramer announced. "One at a time, though. It's not too roomy here. I'll be out of your way. I'm going back to the spacelab module for a while."

"That's great," Joe said. "I'd flip you fellows for it, but we'd never get the coin to come down."

"You go ahead," Frank told him. "Chet and I will fight it out for second place."

"Ah, there's something I'd like to say to you three," Cramer said hesitantly. "There was bad feeling between Stone and Pete McConnel. I didn't feel that way at all. The safety of the *Longeye* project was my only concern."

"We certainly don't blame you for what happened," Frank said.

"Good, I'm glad." Cramer smiled. "If there's anything you'd like to know about *Longeye*, please ask."

"We'll take you up on that," Joe told him.

Cramer floated into the mid-deck compartment, then disappeared through the airlock tunnel on the aft bulkhead.

"See you guys later," Joe said, and pushed himself "up" toward the flight deck.

"Hi, welcome aboard." Major Halman grinned. He sat next to the pilot, Captain Jeff Cooper. Mission Specialist Brett Hilton nodded a greeting. "Take a look," Halman said, "It's something to see."

Instruments and control panels covered all four bulkheads of the flight deck. Joe looked past Halman and peered through the small cabin windows.

"Wow," he said in wonder, "I can't believe I'm really up here!"

"Quite a sight, isn't it?" Captain Cooper said. "We're just passing over the Sinai Peninsula. That's the Nile Valley there, and the Red Sea."

137

The Earth was an incredible shade of cobalt blue and pale gold. Great banks of pure white clouds swept over the land and water. Beyond the curve of the globe, Joe stared into the startling darkness of deep space. The stars were points of cold, unwavering light, their brightness undiminished by the Earth's atmosphere.

"Everything's so—so quiet up here," Joe said. "You can almost hear the silence." He floated back and looked out the small aft windows. The large, curved cargo doors had been opened, and he could see the big cylinder that was the spacelab module, and past it, the aft portion of the cargo bay open to space.

Mission Specialist Brett Hilton floated up to Joe's side. "I saw you in the briefing," he said, "so I imagine you're aware of what we're doing back there. The front section of the spacelab, the pressurized module, is aboard for deep space testing. It's a new, more sophisticated version of the European Space Agency's model. The aft section, the part exposed to outer space, will be aboard on our next flight. Right now, we're using the rear sector of the shuttle's payload area for other experiments—crystal growth, the effect of cosmic particles on certain materials. And, of course, we'll be launching *Longeye* from there."

"That's really what this mission is all about, isn't it?" Joe asked.

Brett Hilton nodded. "We've got some other things going, but yes, *Longeye* is the shuttle's major project."

"Hey," Chet called out, his head suddenly appearing in the flight deck hatch. "Are you going to stay up there all day?"

"Don't worry," Joe told him, "there's an awful lot of space out there. I left plenty for you to see."

15 A Startling Surprise

Several hours into the flight, the Hardys and Chet Morton got a chance to try their first meal in space. Consuming solids was fairly easy, but liquids were a problem. They had to be drunk out of squeeze bottles or containers with straws in the lid. In zero gravity, liquids form droplets and float free—a real danger to the electronic equipment aboard the shuttle.

After lunch, Chet talked with Major Halman on the flight deck. Joe spent several hours with Nat Cramer, learning more about *Longeye*. Frank kept mostly to himself.

The first day in space passed quickly. Though *Skyfire* circled the Earth every two hours, the crew lived by their own "night and day" clock, taking turns in the sleep restraint bags in the mid-deck compartment. The bags were attached to the wall to keep the sleeper from floating about.

Chet liked the idea and dozed off at once. Joe couldn't get used to "lying down standing up," and gave up after a few minutes. He found Frank past the airlock tunnel in the space module. The curved walls were dark except for a pinpoint spot at his brother's shoulder, and the luminous glow of the computer screen before him.

"What are you up to?" Joe asked curiously. "I can tell by that look you've got something on your mind."

"Just doing a little thinking with the space-lab's on-board computer," Frank told him. "No one's using it, and Major Halman said it'd be okay."

Joe squinted at the screen and gave a low whistle through his teeth. "Hey, that's Franz Schacht's criminal record. You've linked up with the computer in our van on Earth!"

"Right," Frank said absently. He paused, and bit his lip in thought. "This case keeps bothering me, Joe. It's just not right. Something's missing."

"I know what you mean," Joe agreed. "But what? We've been over everything a dozen times. It's open and shut. Period."

"I know," Frank said tightly, "and that's

141

what I don't like. Everything's too neat and tidy. Stone and Gorman are practically buried under a ton of evidence."

"Hey, what's going on?" Chet suddenly popped through the tunnel and drifted over to Frank and Joe.

"You kept all that videotape we got on the nightscope, didn't you?" Frank asked.

"Sure," Chet told him. "Why?"

Frank tapped the entry code and watched the eerie red images flick by. "That's the dune buggy when it first appeared," he said. "There—" He froze the vehicle in mid-air, then zoomed in close on the driver and the man with the gun. "Is there any more of this?" he asked Chet.

"No. They were out of sight too fast. I didn't get a thing on the second run. The camera atop the van was at too tight an angle."

"You're trying to check the body characteristics of those guys in the dune buggy, right?" Joe said.

"That's it."

"Fine, but what good will that do now?"

"Just hang on a minute. I want to—" Suddenly, a new set of images appeared on the screen.

"Hey," Chet blurted, "those tapes don't have anything to do with this case!"

"I know," Frank said curiously. "The computer's up to something. Let's see where it's trying to go."

Half an hour later, Frank leaned back and let out a long sigh. There were two pictures on the screen. "The body profile of the dune buggy driver matches that man on the right," he said shakily. "It does; it's the *same* man."

Joe stared at the images in disbelief. "I know it can't be—but it is. Frank, you know what this means, don't you?"

"It means we've got a lot more answers to dig out of this computer," Frank said grimly. "And unless I miss my guess, we're running out of time fast!"

Putting their heads together, the Hardys and Chet Morton came up with a plan they thought might end the mystery once and for all. It was a desperate gamble, but Major Halman agreed to give it a chance. Now, Frank, Joe, and Chet were crowded into the upper compartment to witness the big event, the launching of the *Longeye* satellite.

"I have 1305 hours, 32 seconds," Nat Cramer said.

"Check," Brett Hilton nodded. "*Longeye* launch control ready and holding."

Hilton had already moved the cargo bay's

143

flexible mechanical arm into position. A TV camera attached to the arm relayed an image of the cargo bay to a monitor on his console. At the precise moment, Hilton would lift the *Longeye* satellite out of the bay and set it into orbit.

The minutes crept by. 1314. 1315. 1316.

"Twenty-five seconds to launch," Hilton droned. "Twenty-four. Twenty-three. Twenty-two—"

Suddenly, the lights on the flight deck flickered and went out, plunging the cabin into darkness. Seconds later, the lights returned with a feeble glow.

"What is it, what's wrong?" Cramer turned to face Major Halman.

"Power failure," Halman said calmly. "Don't worry, we'll get everything under control. Brett, put a hold on the launch. We'll have to delay a while."

"Delay?" Cramer blinked. "How long a delay, major? The success of the launching depends on precise timing. We can't—"

"Mr. Cramer," Halman smiled patiently, "we'll work this out. I'll make course corrections and give you another chance."

"Yes, of course," Cramer said dryly. "It won't be long, will it?"

"Not long at all," Halman assured him.

"Major, I'm not too sure of that," Cooper said cautiously. "I've checked everything half a dozen times. We've got a big problem, I'm afraid."

"Great," Halman sighed. "How big, Jeff?"

"Our batteries are losing power fast. We can maintain life support systems. That's about all."

"Uh, what's that mean in plain language?" Joe asked.

"It means we're not going anywhere," Halman said flatly. "We can't generate enough juice to fire our orbital maneuvering engines or thruster rockets. We don't have the power for re-entry. In a word, gentlemen, we're stuck up here until help arrives."

"*Stuck!*" Cramer went pale. "For how long?"

"I'm sure Mission Control can have a rescue shuttle up within a week or so. There's plenty of food and water and air, and—"

"No," Cramer shouted, "we have to launch that satellite. We've got to do it now!"

"Why, Mr. Cramer?" Frank asked. "The major just said we'll be okay. *Longeye* will still be there when they get us repaired and on our way."

Cramer gave a harsh, ragged cry, pushed himself off the aft bulkhead and leaped through the flight deck hatch to the mid-deck compartment below.

Joe pretended to grab for Cramer's leg, making certain he missed. "Okay, he's taking the bait," he grinned once Cramer was out of earshot. "He's crawling through the airlock tunnel to the spacelab module."

Jeff Cooper glanced at his console. "He's closed and secured the airlock door."

"He's going outside," Frank exclaimed, "I *knew* that's what he'd do! He's getting a space suit and going outside!"

"This plan of yours better work," snapped Halman.

"I have a red light on the board," Cooper announced. "He's depressurizing the module."

"I've got him on the monitor," Hilton said suddenly. "There, the airlock atop the spacelab. He's coming out!"

"Major," Frank said, "I have to go after him."

"No, that's impossible." Halman shook his head. "Too dangerous. If anyone's going out, it'll have to be Jeff or me."

"You're right," Frank said, "I don't have the experience. But I do know what to *say* to this character. If he panics out there—"

"All right," Halman muttered. "I don't like

it, but you've got my okay." His gray eyes narrowed with concern. "I don't have to tell you to be careful. You'll only make one mistake in deep space. You won't be around for the second."

Frank opened the airlock door, pulled himself carefully through the hatch and emerged into the cold vacuum of space. He attached his safety line clip to a ring atop the module, turned, and began pulling himself aft toward the cargo bay. Cramer stood thirty feet away, clinging to the shiny bulk of the *Longeye* satellite. His white space suit seemed to glow against the black fabric of space.

"Mr. Cramer, give up," Frank spoke into his helmet mike. "It's over."

"Get away from me," Cramer bellowed. "Don't come any closer!" He braced his feet on the cargo bay floor, grasped the mechanical arm, and tried desperately to tug it free.

"You're wasting your time," Frank said. "There's not enough power on the ship, and you can't possibly do it yourself. You know that."

"I've got to get *Longeye* into space," Cramer raged. "Got to . . . do it . . . now!"

"That satellite's not going anywhere."

"No. That's not true!" Cramer struggled

147

with the giant arm again, pounding it useless-ly with his padded fists. "I'll do it! I've got to—"

Without warning, Frank pushed himself off and hurled through space like a missile. Too late, Cramer turned and raised his arms in alarm. The force of Frank's body shook him free. Cramer screamed in fear.

Frank saw the bright blue curve of the Earth tilting crazily overhead. Suddenly, a hard jolt brought him up short as the safety line tether reached its limit. The force pro-pelled him in a lazy arc back toward the shuttle. He grabbed the line and pulled him-self quickly back to the ship. Cramer was still struggling, shouting and flailing about some forty yards off in deep space. Frank pushed himself back to *Longeye* and grasped Cramer's line.

"Get me back," Cramer yelled. "I can't stand it out here!"

"Tell me what I want to hear or you'll stay out there," Frank said grimly.

"No, don't!" Cramer pleaded.

"Why is it so important to get *Longeye* off the shuttle, Mr. Cramer?"

"I . . . do whatever you like," Cramer blurted, "I won't tell you a thing!"

"Fine. If that's the way you want it." Frank

unhooked the end of Cramer's line and held it in his hand. "Now all I have to do is give you a little shove. You'll float right along with the shuttle for a while. Then you'll start to drift away. Once that happens—"

"No, don't." Cramer screamed, "You—you wouldn't do that."

"*Talk*," Frank demanded. "Right now!"

"All right, all right," Cramer pleaded. "There's an explosive device on *Longeye*. *It's set to go off in half an hour!*"

Frank grinned and let out a long breath. "Okay, major," he said into his mike. "It worked. We're okay."

"What? What are you talking about?" Cramer blurted.

"There's nothing wrong with the shuttle's power," Frank explained. "We just had to make you think there was. Now, you'd better tell me exactly how to dismantle that explosive device."

"Figure it out for yourself, Hardy!" Cramer blurted.

"Okay," Frank said calmly. "Just float around out there until you change your mind. Or until I get tired of holding onto this line!"

16 Questions and Answers

Several days later, the evening sun was setting behind the Hardys' beach house. The remains of hamburgers and potato salad had been cleared from the big picnic table on the patio, where the Hardys and Chet had gathered with Lew Gorman, Suzanne, her father, and Maxwell Grant.

"It was Cramer and McConnel right from the beginning," Frank said. "They planned the whole thing and faked that foreign agent business. Only now, we know they weren't acting alone. There's a lot more to this case than meets the eye."

"It was McConnel's idea to involve Mr. Stone and get him out of the way," Joe put in. "He knew Stone was a danger. And later, when he learned Lew Gorman had worked for a company with suspicious foreign connections, he figured Lew would make a perfect scapegoat, along with Harry Stone."

"They almost got away with it, too," Stone muttered angrily. "They really had us nailed!"

"We've got *them* nailed now," Joe grinned, "right up against the wall."

"I get the shivers just thinking about it," Suzanne said soberly. "They had everything worked out to the letter!"

"They didn't miss a lot," Frank agreed. "That business with the explosion that supposedly endangered *Longeye* was designed to discredit Mr. Stone, and reinforce the story of spies operating right under his nose. McConnel managed to "find" that piece of plastic explosive, and run with it right to Mr. Grant."

"They asked us to that mysterious meeting on the beach," Joe went on, "and called Gorman at the same time. Before he left, they planted the money in his car, for insurance, in case any of us survived that dune buggy attack."

"It was McConnel, of course, who arranged the foreign agent story, right?" Mr. Hardy asked.

"Right, Dad," Frank answered. "He was formerly with army intelligence, remember? He simply got hold of the records of a real agent who hadn't been seen for a couple of years. That started us off on the Franz Schacht story. They got a real break when we found Gorman burying that mask of Schacht. Of course, if we hadn't caught him with it, they would have made sure it was discovered some other way."

"Those prints on the dune buggy," Chet said, "that was a pretty smart trick. Now that we know the real Franz Schacht was never around, the police have re-examined that print and learned it was applied by a special carbon process. It was Schacht's fingerprint all right, but he didn't put it there. McConnel got it from his records."

"They worked the Schacht business well," Mr. Hardy said. "Gorman was with you during the dune buggy attack, when they left the print for us to find. Later, they made us believe Gorman was wearing the Schacht mask when McConnel was supposedly shot. We had a real Schacht print and a fake Schacht as well. That reinforced McConnel's plot to make us think the real Schacht was trying to confuse us—when he never was anywhere near here!"

"Then there never was a foreign agent loose in NASA." Maxwell Grant sighed.

"Not a one," Frank told him. "The man who tried to kill Joe in the centrifuge was Cramer. He also put the hallucinogenic crystals in Chet's airhose. And it was Cramer who "shot" Pete McConnel in front of the Champs Élysées restaurant. He slipped out of his car at the curb, put on his Franz Schacht mask, fired at McConnel, circled the back of the restaurant and came running up to "help" McConnel, who had broken a fake blood capsule inside his shirt."

"And I got the blame for it," Gorman said darkly. "It was pretty smart, all right. Who'd ever suspect the shooting was a fake?"

"They used another mask to finally convince us," Joe said. "They made dead certain we thought we saw Harry Stone trying to kill us with a sub-machine gun. That was really Cramer, of course. And McConnel was on hand to make sure Mr. Stone had two flat tires, so he couldn't account for his time while we were being attacked. With Stone and Gorman both behind bars, Cramer and McConnel were free to go ahead with their scheme."

"This is the part I still don't believe!" Suzanne shook her head in wonder. "They pretended they were so worried about something happening to their company's project, and all the time they were planning to steal it for themselves!"

"They nearly pulled it off, too," Joe said somberly. "We weren't convinced Stone and Gorman were guilty, but Cramer and McConnel had done an awesome job of setting them up for a frame. Then, aboard *Skyfire,* Frank started putting some of his famous hunches into the computer."

"I just did a little double-checking on the data we had," Frank said evenly. "I tried to get a body characteristic match up, using the dune buggy videotapes as a base. That was when the computer threw us a big surprise. It found a match, all right, but the source of that match really tossed us into a spin. The computer had nightscope videos in its banks of the men who attacked us in the Okefenokee Swamp, and later, shots of the people who went after Dad on the beach. Bingo! One of the men who attacked us in Okefenokee was also the driver of that dune buggy!"

"We thought the computer had gone crazy," Joe said. "Dad's case had nothing to do with ours. Yet, there was obviously a connection. The industrial thieves Dad was after were somehow involved with the trouble at

NASA. That meant they were after something valuable."

"And the *Longeye* radio telescope was the obvious answer," Mr. Hardy finished.

"Exactly," Frank said. "It had to be. And McConnel and Cramer were the men closest to *Longeye*. What if they'd made a deal with this international ring? I followed up another hunch just to make sure we were on the right track. Using our link to the computer in our van, I checked out hospital emergency room records for the night Mr. McConnel was supposedly shot. There was *no* record of McConnel showing up for treatment, anywhere. Even if he'd gone to a private doctor, that doctor would have had to notify the police about a gunshot wound. So, if McConnel was really shot, what was he hiding? And if he wasn't, that told us all we needed to know."

"Dad's run down most of the industrial thieves who were working with Cramer and McConnel," Joe said, "and we know the ring has no loyalty to any nation or political system. They steal the world's secrets, and sell them to the highest bidder."

"Now that Cramer and McConnel have told their story," Joe added, "we know they'd made a deal to sell *Longeye* for four million bucks."

"Wow!" Suzanne exclaimed. "That's a lot of money!"

"It sure is," Frank said. "But it would have been a real bargain for the industrial thieves. The sophisticated technology in *Longeye* is almost priceless."

"The only trouble was," Harry Stone mused, "*Longeye* was under heavy security at NASA. Even though Cramer and McConnel were with the Starglass Corporation, they couldn't risk hauling off the entire instrument package. That would have been too risky."

"Once we decided those two were involved," Frank said, "we had a pretty good idea how they planned to pull it off. There was a mock-up of *Longeye*, remember? The answer was to install the fake *Longeye* in the shuttle. Cramer had it set to explode an hour after it was launched. Stone and Gorman were in jail on Earth. They'd probably get the blame, along with the mythical Schacht and his non-existent spy ring. Meanwhile, McConnel would get the real *Longeye* out of NASA, labeled as a mock-up, of course, and turn it over to the industrial spies. If anyone asked about the mock-up later, Cramer could say he dismantled it in the Starglass labs, trying to 'find' what went wrong with the satellite that exploded!"

"Major Halman was glad to go along with our bluff," Frank grinned, "after we explained the situation."

"Did you know Cramer planned to blow up the *Longeye* package?" Suzanne asked.

"I didn't know for sure, but I had a good idea the *Longeye* aboard *Skyfire* had to be a fake. That meant Cramer couldn't risk letting it stay in orbit too long. Instruments on Earth would see it wasn't working, and the next shuttle that went up would haul it in for repairs. And that would be the end of Cramer's scheme."

"So you forced his hand," Maxwell Grant said. "He had to go outside and try to get that satellite off of the shuttle."

"He knew that was impossible—he wasn't thinking straight. He panicked; he had to do something."

"Do you think he would have let the explosive device go off if you hadn't tried to stop him?" Gorman asked curiously. "Would he have let himself go up with the shuttle and everyone aboard, to keep from being exposed?"

"I don't know," Frank said thoughtfully, gazing out at the flat expanse of the Atlantic.

"I don't think I want to know. Fortunately, when I got him out at the end of that line, he was more frightened of floating off in space than he was of going to jail or getting blown up."

"You wouldn't have *really* let him go, would you?" Suzanne asked.

"No, of course not," Frank grinned. "He didn't know that, though, did he?"

"Lucky for us," Chet said solemnly.

"Hey, Chet," Frank said dryly, "you didn't have any doubts that he'd crack, did you?"

"I *don't* think I'm going to answer that," Chet said.

"Okay," Joe laughed, "that's enough talk for today. Anyone ready for a swim? I'll race you to, ah—Bermuda and back, Chet."

"Forget it," Chet growled. "I've had all the weightless fun I can take for awhile. I'm staying right in this chair on the good old solid Earth!"